And I kissed him back.

I was in his arms. His lips were on mine. The world around us disappeared. There was no one here but me. And Mike. I held him tight. Mike's mouth was warm and soft on mine. My legs were like rubber. I held him tighter to keep from falling down.

The DJ started playing Michael Jackson's *Thriller*, and the spell was broken. I backed up from Mike. What had I done? I'd been kissing Mike! He smiled at me. I just stood there. What had I done?

I turned from him and fled. I left the dance floor and headed straight to the bathroom. I splashed water on my face.

What had that been? That kiss had reached down into my insides and pulled. Wow. I splashed more water on my face.

But it was Mike.

Biker Mike.

What was I thinking? I was dating Trevor. What if Trevor had seen us? What if anyone had seen us? Someone must have seen us. We were there in the middle of the dance floor. Sucking face. Oh, my gosh. Someone had to have seen us. It was a small school. I knew everyone. Trevor knew everyone. Someone would tell Trevor. What would I tell Trevor when he asked me about it? He was sure to ask me about it.

I turned my back to the mirror and leaned against the counter. What was I going to do? I couldn't stay in here all night. Okay. Deep breath. It was simple really. I needed to go out there and pretend that it had never happened. I had not kissed Mike. I couldn't have. So it simply must not have happened.

When Mike Kissed Emma

by

Christine Marciniak

This is a work of fiction. Names, characters, places, and incidents either are the product of the author's imagination or are used fictitiously, and any resemblance to actual persons living or dead, business establishments, events, or locales, is entirely coincidental.

When Mike Kissed Emma

Contact Information: info@thewildrosepress.com

Cover Art by *Kim Mendoza*

The Wild Rose Press
PO Box 708
Adams Basin, NY 14410-0706
Visit us at www.thewildrosepress.com

Publishing History
First Climbing Rose Edition, 2009
Print ISBN 1-60154-545-2

Published in the United States of America

Acknowledgements

"The Sound Of Music"
"Sixteen Going On Seventeen"
"Maria"
"My Favorite Things"
"Do-Re-Mi"
"The Lonely Goatherd"
"How Can Love Survive?"1960
"So Long, Farewell"
"Climb Ev'ry Mountain"
"An Ordinary Couple"1960
"Edelweiss"1959
Written by Richard Rodgers &
Oscar Hammerstein II

Dedication

To Adrian - because when he kissed me, everything changed.

Praise for When Mike Kissed Emma

"*When Mike Kissed Emma* is delicious. Christine Marciniak does a magnificent job capturing the rollercoaster which is teenage love. I wanted to be Emma. I wanted to live in her shoes, even just for a day. *When Mike Kissed Emma* has it all. Mystery. Intrigue. Jealousy. And of course the kiss. And trust me when I say a guy like Mike is something we all daydream about."

~PJ Hoover, author of *The Emerald Tablet.*

Chapter 1
"My Heart Wants to Sing Every Song it Hears"

I walked right into him. I didn't even see him standing there until I bounced off his chest. Books went flying. Pencils and pens clattered across the black and white floor tiles. And I would have landed on the floor, too, if he hadn't grabbed my arms and steadied me. I looked up to thank him and saw the most gorgeous blue eyes. Really blue. I'd never seen anyone with eyes that blue. But then I saw who those eyes belonged to.

Biker Mike.

I took a step back and disengaged myself from his hands. Biker Mike wasn't your typical St. Stephen's student. He looked more like a public school student with his long hair, untucked shirt, and sleeves rolled up to show off his tattoo. He also wore a leather jacket whenever he didn't have to be strictly in uniform. No one I knew had become friends with him since he transferred here this year. He came and went every day on his beat-up old motorcycle. He could be a drug dealer or in a gang, for all I knew. It wouldn't do to get too close to him.

"You should watch where you're going," he said, sounding more amused than annoyed.

"Sorry," I bent down to pick up my scattered belongings. The love poem Trevor had passed to me this afternoon was sticking out of my notebook. I shoved it back in before anyone else could see it.

Biker Mike bent down to help me. He gathered my pens and handed them to me.

There was a French Lit book on the floor in front of me—not mine. It must belong to him. I handed it over, and he passed me my Trig book.

"Well, thanks." I stood up again.

"No problem. I hope you didn't miss your bus."

"Oh." That was sweet. "I wasn't rushing to get the bus. I'm on my way to auditions." I tapped a nearby poster. It was one Caitlyn had made with lots of glitter and a picture of a nun doing an Uncle Sam imitation: I want you to try out for *The Sound of Music.*

"You're the school play type, huh?" He leaned against a nearby locker and looked at me through narrowed eyes.

And what type was that? I stood up straighter under his scrutiny. I didn't know what went on at his old school, but here school plays were a big deal. There was even a Broadway actress who could trace her start to a St. Stephen's school play.

"I was Jean in *Brigadoon* last year," I said, my chin held high, "and this year I'm going to be Liesl." I looked down the hall toward my locker. I still had to get there before going to the theater and I didn't want to be late.

"I thought you said you were *going* to auditions." Mike smiled as he handed me one more pencil he'd picked up off the floor.

"Yeah, so?" I took the pencil from him. "Thanks."

"Don't they usually choose the parts after the auditions, not before?"

Oh. Well. Blood rushed to my cheeks. "I have confidence," I said, quoting one of the songs from the movie. Besides, it wasn't like I wanted the lead or anything.

"I see." And he looked me up and down as if he were seeing a whole lot more than I thought I was showing.

"Emma, come on." Caitlyn, her sleek black ponytail bouncing behind her, grabbed my arm as if she expected to drag me bodily to auditions. "We're gonna be late."

"Don't pull her arm out of its socket." My other best friend, Lauren, was there too, her straight brown hair falling into a slight curve in front of her face. Her eyes shone as she smiled at me. "We know Emma wouldn't miss auditions."

"I was on my way to my locker, but I kind of ran into Mike here." I looked up, but Biker Mike was already fading into the after school crush of the hall.

"Not Biker Mike?" Lauren said, eyebrows up, her books protectively held in front of her.

"Yeah. I bumped into him."

"It was probably some sort of a snatch and grab pick-pocket operation. Do you still have your wallet?" Caitlyn asked.

"He didn't take my wallet," I said as I continued to my locker. "And besides, *I* ran into *him*." I started to spin the dial on my lock. Please let it open. I didn't want to be any later than I already was.

Lauren leaned against the locker next to mine. She knew it could take me a while to get my locker open. Caitlyn bounced on the balls of her feet. "How are we going to celebrate when you two score the big roles?" she asked.

I looked at Lauren and she grinned at me. We'd had pretty good parts last year as sophomores. And last year's leads had graduated. We had it all planned out. I, of course, would be Liesl, and Lauren, with her background of summer theater camps, would play the part of Maria. I'd already started calling her "mom."

"Cheesy Fries at the Snack Shack." I told Caitlyn.

"That's not a celebration." Caitlyn wrinkled her nose. "That's what we do every day."

I got to the last number in my combination. But, naturally, the lock didn't open. I started over from the beginning.

Lauren sighed.

"I'll get it, just give me a minute," I insisted.

Luckily, it opened on the next try. After all, I had a play to try out for.

I grabbed my backpack and coat and slammed the offending locker shut.

"Maybe if you were nicer to it, it would be nicer to you," Caitlyn said.

"Whatever. You're trying out for the play, right Caitlyn?" I asked as we headed toward the theater.

"Yeah. Why not? Probably another year in the chorus for me. Though, with my luck, I'll be cast as a nun." She snapped her gum. "I don't think I could handle that."

"The world is definitely not ready for you as a nun," Lauren agreed.

I laughed and looked at Caitlyn, with her uniform skirt worn practically as a micro-mini and her bright red lipstick.

When we got to the auditorium, the doors were open, with a steady stream of people going in to audition. Outside the door, leaning slumped against the wall was my sister Sara, her backpack by her feet, her knee socks down around her ankles.

"Hey," I greeted her. "Let's go inside. We need to sign in and everything." I was glad to see her here. This morning she had seemed unsure about trying out. It was just nervousness—fear of failure and all that. She had a great voice, so I knew she would do well in auditions, if she could just get over her stage fright.

"I'm only here because Jake is my ride and it's ten degrees out there. I'm not walking home."

"That's fine." I took hold of Sara's arm to propel her into the room.

"I'm not auditioning," Sara protested.

"The way to overcome fear is to do what you fear. Kind of like getting back on a horse after a fall. Anyway, as long as you're here you might as well audition."

"I'm not afraid, Emma," Sara insisted, pulling

her arm free from my grasp.

But I ignored her and added her name under mine on the sign-up sheet right inside the door. A little nudge was all she needed to bring her out of her shell, and as her big sister, I was the perfect one to provide the nudge.

I took two audition packets and handed one to Sara. She jammed it in her coat pocket without looking at it.

"There you are, Em." Trevor came up to me and put his hand on my hip.

I looked up and brushed his blond hair out of his eyes.

He smiled at me, revealing straight teeth and a dimple in his left cheek. "*You wait little girl on an empty stage*," he sang softly in my ear. That was from "Sixteen Going on Seventeen." That was going to be our song when I got the role of Liesl and Trevor got the role of Rolf, the telegram-carrying boyfriend. He would sing that song to me on stage.

"Let's find a place to sit," I said. But Lauren had apparently scoped out the room because she headed up the aisle with a quick "come on" look over her shoulder. We followed her, and I found myself sitting in the same row as my brother Jake and his friend Justin.

"Took you guys long enough," Jake said.

"I couldn't get into my locker." I stuck my backpack under the seat and my coat over the back of it.

"Forget your numbers again?" Jake asked.

I rolled my eyes. I did not feel like being teased by my brother. Why did Lauren have to pick here to sit? Other than the fact that she had a huge crush on my brother; which I totally couldn't relate to. But apparently I was the only one, because all the girls in the school seemed to love Jake. And on a purely objective level, I'd admit he was good looking, with tousled brown hair and a quirky smile. He was also really talented. My money was on him getting the role of the Captain in this show. Which, of course, was why Lauren wanted to be Maria; all to get my brother. Go figure.

"Yeah, once I learn to count I should be fine," I said and sat down. Lauren was in the seat between us.

"Break a leg, Jake," she said, tossing her hair over her shoulder.

He smiled at her. "That would be inconvenient, wouldn't it?" Then he leaned forward and grinned at me. He didn't have to say anything; I knew just what he was thinking. I actually did break my leg in eighth grade by falling off a stage. People just wish me good luck now. It seems safer.

Jake spotted Sara on the other side of Trevor and Caitlyn. "So, you decided to try out after all?" he asked.

She sank back into the seat. "I don't know why I'm here."

I gave her my brightest smile. "Because you want to feel the glory of being on stage; you want to know the high you can get from hearing the applause of the audience."

She didn't smile back. "It's because you made me come, I'd rather be playing soccer."

"There's no soccer in the winter," I reminded her. I turned my attention to the audition packet.

The song for the girls was "Climb Ev'ry Mountain." I crumpled the paper into a ball and waved it at Lauren. "Why did she choose this song?"

Lauren shrugged. "Maybe because if you can sing this one, you can sing pretty much any of the others." Naturally Lauren wasn't worried, she could sing anything.

"I wish she'd chosen something else. 'Sixteen Going on Seventeen' would have been perfect."

Lauren rolled her eyes. "Yeah, because that's all you've been singing for the past two weeks."

Mrs. Valente, her flowery caftan billowing around her, was up on the stage now, tapping the microphone to get attention. The resulting feedback made everyone wince. "Sorry," she said.

You'd think that for someone who directed plays, she'd have that microphone thing down.

"Let us begin. The audition song will be 'Climb Ev'ry Mountain' for the girls, and 'Edelweiss' for the boys. You will also see in your packets that I've chosen a scene between Maria and the Captain for you to read. Okay." She picked up her sign-up sheet and called the first two students.

Justin and Caitlyn were the first from our group to be called. Caitlyn bounced up to the stage, while Justin stepped on my toes, and everyone else's, in his attempt to get out to the aisle. Once situated, they read the scene together. And if Maria was supposed to be a perky cheerleader and the Captain, a computer geek, they would have had the parts nailed. Justin sang his song competently, but so softly he was impossible to hear. Caitlyn belted out "Climb Ev'ry Mountain" for all she was worth, but the high notes were totally beyond her. I tried not to wince as she strove for them.

Next Jake and Lauren got called up. Lauren gave me a thumbs up. This was a dream come true for her, to be on stage opposite Jake. Maybe she really would get her wish and the two of them would get the lead roles in the play and a romance would be born. A romance like mine and Trevor's. I reached out and held his hand.

The chemistry crackled between them as they read their lines. They should really get the lead roles. They'd be perfect as the Captain and Maria.

If Trevor and I got to go up together, Mrs. Valente could see that we had chemistry too, and she would see that the only logical thing to do would be to cast us in the roles of Liesl and Rolf.

I wanted to do that dancing in the gazebo scene.

And I wanted to do it with Trevor.

I would gracefully leap from bench to bench, with Trevor hanging onto my outstretched—

Trevor stood up and started to inch past me.

"She called you?" I asked, coming back to the humdrum world of the auditorium.

"Yes."

"Who else did she call?" Had I missed her calling my name?

"I don't know. Some freshman." Trevor headed up to the stage.

It wasn't perfect, but still, just because we didn't try out together didn't mean we wouldn't get cast in those roles.

Sara fidgeted in her seat, turning to see who else was here. She made a snorting noise and leaned past both Caitlyn and Trevor's empty seats. "You'll never believe who's here."

"Shhh. Trevor's about to sing."

"No, wait. Biker Mike is here."

Biker Mike? Was at auditions? This should be interesting.

"Can you believe it?" Sara said. "I mean he's like a hoodlum. What would he be doing here? Can you just imagine him in *The Sound of Music*? What would he play? A Nazi?"

I waved my hand to shush Sara. Trevor was singing and I didn't want to miss a note. He sang "Edelweiss" with such warmth and feeling, it gave me goosebumps. Trevor came back off the stage and sat down next to me. "You were great," I told him, and gave him a quick kiss. "The perfect Rolf."

"We'll see if Mrs. Valente agrees with you."

I leaned back in my seat. "How could she not?"

"Did you see that Biker Mike is here?" Trevor asked and chuckled a little. "I don't know why he's even bothering. I mean, this obviously isn't his thing."

I shared his laugh. "I know." But really, I didn't

know what Biker Mike's thing was. I didn't know anything about him, except he took French and had beautiful eyes.

Mrs. Valente called Sara's name. Sara seemed to shrink back into her seat, as if she were trying to make herself invisible. I reached over and nudged her. "Come on, Sara, go on up."

"No," Sara said.

"Yes. You can't be worse than some of the people who've already gone."

"I never said I couldn't do it, I'm just not sure I want to," she hissed at me. But she headed to the stage.

I felt a little thrill of satisfaction for her. After all, Jake and I were in lots of plays and we loved it.

"Wow. Sara can really sing," Trevor whispered to me as Sara started belting out "Climb Ev'ry Mountain." I noticed she had her eyes closed, but I could work on stage presence with her later.

"I know. Why do you think I wanted her to audition?"

She was good, too, reading the lines. She should definitely be on stage. Mrs. Valente better agree.

"Thank you, Sara, Ryan. Now let's have Emma Landon and Mike Anderson."

Mike Anderson? Ugh. Biker Mike! I had to audition with Biker Mike. That totally sucked, because how was Mrs. Valente really going to see how well I could read the scene if my partner was horrible. It wasn't fair. It really wasn't.

"Good luck," Lauren said to me as I headed up to the stage.

I had to sing first. I wish it were any other song in *The Sound of Music*, but if I wanted to prove what I could do, than sing it I must. So I sang it like I was the Mother Abbess sending poor novice Maria out into the cruel world.

I nailed it.

Then Biker Mike sang. He sounded like that kid

in *High School Musical*. No kidding. He had a voice that could be on Broadway. How could a voice like that be attached to a person who looked like a street thug? He even needed a shave, for goodness' sake.

I was staring at him, mouth open. Uncool. I shut my mouth. I bet he sings in the shower. I shook my head. Better not even go there!

Then it was time for Biker Mike and me to read the lines. I'd heard them read so many times that I knew them by heart. I didn't even need the piece of paper, so I just started.

It was the scene leading up to their romantic song: the scene where the Captain and Maria start to realize that they have fallen in love with each other. I had the first line.

"*I'm sorry if I said something I shouldn't have said.*" I looked straight into those incredible blue eyes.

Biker Mike said the next line, looking right back into my eyes. "*You did say the wrong thing, but you said it at the right time.*"

It felt like he was seeing deep into my soul. I shivered a little and almost stumbled on the next line.

We read through the scene, right up to Biker Mike reading, "*When you were a very little girl, did a very little boy ever kiss you?*"

My heart was beating faster, as if I were really Maria anticipating a kiss from the Captain.

Who was this person standing opposite me?

He looked like Biker Mike. But he couldn't be.

It was like standing up here with Captain Von Trapp. He even seemed like he looked different, but he still had the long hair, the tattoo, the leather jacket.

What was different?

I read my line, "*Uh-huh*"

And Biker Mike moved closer, looked into my eyes with those incredible blue ones of his, and said

"*That's quite different too.*"

And luckily the scene ended there. Because I was beginning to want to be kissed by the person with those great blue eyes. But, I mean, the last thing I want is to be kissed by Biker Mike. Right?

"Thank you, Emma, Mike," Mrs. Valente said, and broke the spell.

I left the stage quickly, not even looking back.

My friends all had their coats on already. Now that we had done our bit we could go. Tomorrow Mrs. Valente would post the callback list. Then we'd have to try out again—for specific parts.

Once we were out of the theater, Lauren said, "You did a great job up there. You're a shoe-in for Liesl."

"I sure hope so."

"And Biker Mike. He has unexpected talents," Caitlyn added.

Yeah. He did. Didn't he? I looked over my shoulder, but I didn't see him anywhere.

"You guys looked good together," Sara said with a smirk.

As if! Long hair, leather jacket, tattoo—hardly my ideal guy. I moved closer to Trevor. And he casually put his arm over my shoulder. He was my ideal. I didn't want anyone getting the wrong idea.

Chapter 2
"Catch a Cloud and Pin it Down"

The list was posted by lunchtime.

"I'm in." Sara's eyes were wide with a look of disbelief as she leaned on the locker next to mine, her books clasped in front of her.

"In what?" I asked, as I fidgeted with the dial on my lock.

"The play. I'm on the callback list."

Ha! I knew she could do it if she tried. She ought to listen to me more often. "That's wonderful news, Sara. Who else is on the list?" I turned the dial to the last number and pulled on the latch. It didn't open.

Sigh.

"Didn't you look at it?" Sara asked.

"Not yet." I tried the lock again. "Who else got in?"

"I didn't read the whole darn list," Sara said, "but you and Jake are on it, and so are Lauren, Caitlyn, and Trevor."

This was going to be such a great play. I remembered Biker Mike's awesome singing. Had he got in? "And Biker Mike?" I asked Sara, studying the folders and books that I was holding, instead of looking at her.

"Dunno. Wasn't looking for him. Better if he's not anyway. He's kind of scary." She watched me pointlessly spin the dial on my lock for a moment. "Well, I'm going," she said, finally. "Good luck with the locker."

Lauren and Caitlyn appeared almost as soon as Sara left. "Open that locker already," Lauren said. "I want to check the callback lists before lunch."

"We made it," I said as I got to the last number. For good measure I gave my locker a punch and it opened. I'd have to remember that technique.

"You checked the list?" Caitlyn asked with a little bounce.

"Sara did. You guys, me, Trevor, and Jake—and Sara. We're all in."

"We made callbacks?" Trevor asked, coming up from behind me and putting his arm around me.

"But of course." I flashed him a bright smile, retrieved my lunch, and shut my locker. "Come on. Let's go eat."

We sat at our usual table, and I took out my peanut butter and jelly sandwich.

"You ever going to branch out and try something different for lunch?" Lauren asked, as she flipped her hair over her shoulder and unwrapped a granola bar.

"If it ain't broken, don't fix it," I said and took a bite. Lauren had been making fun of my lunch choice for years now, ever since she'd decided, at nine, that she was too mature for peanut butter and jelly.

"Très cliché," Caitlyn said.

I shrugged, popped open a Diet Coke, and took a sip. Out of the corner of my eye, I saw Biker Mike sitting at a table with a couple of other juniors. He was sitting apart though, a crumpled paper bag in front of him, a can of Dr. Pepper in his hand. Had he gotten called back too? If I had checked the list myself I would have known. I could go over there and ask. It's not like he was talking to the other people at his table. But how could I explain to Lauren and Caitlyn that I wanted to talk to Biker Mike? More importantly, how could I explain it to Trevor? I guess I'd just have to wait and see if he was at callbacks.

"What do you think, Emma?" Trevor asked.

"About what?" Had I really been so busy watching Biker Mike that I'd been ignoring Trevor?

Lauren laughed. "Her head is so in the clouds over thoughts of being Leisl that she didn't even hear you."

Trevor smiled indulgently. "Do you think Jake will get the part of the Captain?"

I shrugged. "Why wouldn't he? He's a senior. He's good." I grinned at Lauren. "Then you can be Maria and spend all kinds of wonderful time falling in love with him."

She smiled dreamily. "That would be awesome."

****

The last bell rang. I couldn't wait to get to callbacks. The part of Liesl was practically mine. I knew it was. I just had to do a good job today and I'd have the part I'd been dreaming about for years.

"Emma! Wait up!" I turned to see Sara rushing to catch up with me and Lauren and Caitlyn as we headed toward our lockers.

We all stopped. Sara had a wild look in her eyes. "I can't do it, Emma," she said.

I sighed. Time for another pep talk. I turned to Lauren and Caitlyn. "You guys go ahead. I'll meet you in the auditorium." Then I pulled Sara into the nearest classroom. "What's the problem?" I perched on the edge of a desk.

Sara paced back and forth in front of me. "Auditions were okay. We all had to do the same stuff and some people were really bad, like Justin." She giggled a little then continued, "But this is different. Everyone that's going to be there today is going to be good."

"Right," I said. "And so are you. That's why you're there."

"What if I make a fool of myself?" She turned to the whiteboard, grabbed a marker, and started doodling. "What if I get up there and they realize that I'm no good. That yesterday was a fluke."

"Then you get a part in the chorus," I said and watched her draw a little person clutching his heart and falling off a stage.

"Besides, I don't think I want to be in a school play," she said, erasing her drawing and turning back to me.

"How do you know unless you try?" How could I convince her that she did have talent and she was going to have fun? I'd already told her countless times. "Listen, Sara, you don't have to give a Broadway-quality performance. Get up there today, do your best, and Mrs. Valente will decide what role is best for you. Freshmen don't usually get major roles anyway. You'll maybe get to be one of the nuns or the maid or something—if you get a talking part at all. It won't be a lot of pressure or stress and you'll get to see what it's all about. If you don't like it, don't do it next year. But at least give it a chance."

"You mean I might get a part where I hardly have to talk?"

"Probably a part without any lines at all." I jumped down from the desk and put my arm around her. "My freshman year I was a flower seller in *My Fair Lady*. No lines." I led her toward the door. "No worries, okay? Just enjoy."

She took a deep breath and exhaled noisily. "I guess it could be okay if I didn't have any lines."

"That's the spirit," I said and we headed into the hall. "I still have to go to my locker. I'll meet you there." I headed down the hall and crossed my fingers that she would actually appear in the auditorium.

The halls were already emptying for the afternoon. I turned the dial on my locker and, naturally, when I got to the last number, nothing happened. I tried again. No luck. I tried giving it a swift kick, but it didn't work.

"Need help there?" It was Biker Mike, at his

locker, a couple of feet away.

"Um, no. I've got it," I said.

"Clearly." He came over to me. "On your way to callbacks?"

"That's the plan," I said shortly as I tried my combination again. It failed. Again.

"What's your combination?" Biker Mike asked.

"We're not supposed to give out that information." As if I was going to give my combination to Biker Mike. He might be a great singer, but he still looked like the kind of guy who might stash drugs in there or something.

"I'm not going to steal your Algebra book," he said. "I just want to help you out."

I blushed. I might not trust him, but I didn't want him to know that. "I take Trig."

"I don't want that book either," he assured.

Luckily the locker opened this time. "Thanks anyway." I stashed the books I didn't need and grabbed my coat.

Mike fell into step beside me as I headed to the auditorium. "Are you going to callbacks too?" I asked, though it seemed kind of obvious, since he was walking that way.

"Yeah," he said.

We walked toward the auditorium in awkward silence. Conversation seemed called for. "You were good at auditions yesterday."

"You too," he responded. "You're sure to get Liesl, like you want."

"I bet you'll get a good role too," I said. He could be…who? Jake would be the Captain, Trevor would be Rolf. Maybe Max? That would be a good role for Mike.

"I hope so." We walked the rest of the way in silence. "Break a leg," he said as we entered the theater and went our own ways.

He didn't know about the taboo against saying that to me.

"Yeah. Thanks. You too." I went to find Trevor and my friends.

They were all seated in the front row. Sara was there too. "My locker is the bane of my existence," I said as I draped my coat over the back of the chair. "Even giving it a good swift kick didn't help, and then," I said, and sat down, "Biker Mike wanted me to give him my locker combination so he could help me."

"You didn't give it to him, did you?" Trevor asked, scrunching up his forehead in that cute way he does when he's worried.

"Of course not. Can you imagine what could have happened if I did? It could lead to drug raids, bomb sniffing dogs, the possibilities are endless. And frightening." I shuddered at the very thought. Though, actually, Mike seemed kind of nice when I talked to him. Maybe he did just want to help.

Trevor put his arm around me. "I think you need a certain amount of drama in your life to keep you going."

Hmph. Trevor was wrong. I didn't need drama in my life. What I needed was being on stage. I needed the applause. The attention. I frowned. Was that a bad reflection on me, that I required attention? No. If I needed everyone's attention all the time, that would be bad. I just wanted it when I was on stage. That was fine. I nestled against Trevor and waited for my destiny to unfold.

Okay, maybe I liked a bit of drama in my life.

Mrs. Valente got us to settle down and immediately began calling people up to read different parts. I waited patiently for my chance to show what I could do as Liesl. In the meantime, I had to endure other people playing Liesl, and had to read for other characters as well.

Finally Mrs. Valente said, "Emma, will you read the part of Liesl on page thirty-nine, and Trevor, you take the part of Rolf."

Yes. I pumped my fist as I stood up. What could be more perfect than this? Now Mrs. Valente was going to see how well we would do in the parts.

I took Trevor's hand as we climbed the steps to the stage. This was the start of something wonderful. We'd get to do this scene over and over in rehearsal. We'd get to sing a romantic song to each other and look deep into each other's eyes—and Jake wouldn't even be able to tease me about public displays of affection, because it would all be part of the script. Ha.

I had the first line. *"Good night, Rolf."*

Trevor looked at his script and then up at me. He smiled. *"Liesl!"*

I said my next line and he said his. He was doing a fine job of reading the part of Rolf. But it was weird. I couldn't say why, but something wasn't clicking. Not like it had yesterday when I was reading with Mike. This kept being me and Trevor. It didn't change into Liesl and Rolf. That made no sense. Those parts were ideal for us. We *were* Liesl and Rolf. Not that Trevor was a closet Nazi or anything, but I was sixteen going on seventeen, and we were in love.

Why did it just feel like we were simply reading the lines to each other? Where was the chemistry? We needed that chemistry. It couldn't fail me now; this was the moment of truth, the one chance we had to show what we could do.

"Okay, thank you. Trevor, stay where you are. And Sara, will you please come up and read the part of Liesl?"

I swallowed a lump in my throat as I stepped off the stage. Had I blown it? My one shot at my dream part and it was over? Had I managed to convince Mrs. Valente that I was perfect for the part?

Sara mumbled something under her breath as we passed and she made her way up to the stage where Trevor waited for her. I sat down to watch.

Sara was nervous as she read the part. But in a funny way, it worked for the scene. He was so gentle and tender with her, as if he really cared about her. And when she said, *"You're wonderful"* to him, she sounded so much like a girl with her first boyfriend that it was a bit eerie

After they read, Mrs. Valente called me and Jake up to read as the Captain and Maria.

"Mrs. Valente," I said. "You know you can't cast us in these parts." I mean, I was not playing a part where I had to marry my brother. No how. No way.

"I just want to see how you read the parts," Mrs. Valente assured.

Okay. That was fine then. We read the scene where Maria first meets the Captain and he looks her over and is less-than-impressed with the way she is dressed. He tells her to change her clothes before she meets the children.

As Jake said it to me, it felt so much like "big brother" Jake making some comment about what I was wearing on a date that I wanted to laugh. And then, when Maria tells the Captain that she doesn't have any other dresses because her worldly dresses were given to the poor—except the one she was wearing, because even the poor rejected it, Jake made such a face that I almost did burst out laughing. I think Jake has a calling as a comedic actor.

And I know there was no chemistry there—no romantic chemistry anyway.

Once everyone had a turn, Mrs. Valente sat with her assistant and consulted her notes. All we could do was wait. Sara was texting someone, Lauren and Caitlyn were whispering and giggling, and I tapped my foot nervously until Trevor put his hand on my knee to stop my fidgeting.

I looked at him and smiled. "I want to dance that incredible dance in the gazebo with you, running from bench to bench."

"I think the dance is only in the movie, not the play," Trevor said, thumbing through the script.

That just wasn't fair.

Finally, Mrs. Valente took the stage. "Settle down people," she called, ineffectually. She clapped her hands. Still a dull roar could be heard in the auditorium. Her assistant went over to the piano and pounded on as many keys as she could at once. That got people's attention.

She began with the chorus and the nuns. Caitlyn got a role as a nun, which made the rest of us laugh out loud. Then Mrs. Valente worked her way up to the lead roles, kind of like at the Miss America pageant, they announced the runners up first. Students from the grade school next door were playing the younger children. There were sighs and cheers as people found out what parts they would be playing. Soon she was up to the part of Rolf, the telegram-delivering boyfriend of Liesl.

"Rolf will be played by Trevor McGrath."

"Yes!" I shouted, as Trevor sat smiling quietly by my side. Oops. Fortunately she moved on quickly to other parts.

"The part of Liesl," Mrs. Valente said—I got ready to shout out again, "will be played by Sara Landon."

"Yes!"

Wait.

What did she say?

Sara.

Sara Landon.

Not Emma Landon.

There must be some mistake.

That part is mine.

That part isn't for Sara. Sara didn't even want to be in the play. She just wanted to play soccer. I couldn't believe it. I convinced her to be in the play and she stole my part. Sara just sat in silence, her mouth forming a stunned O.

Now Mrs. Valente was announcing Mother Abbess. Please don't let me get the part of Mother Abbess. I don't want that role. I really don't want that role. I will cry if I get that role, and I don't want to cry in front of everyone.

I want to be Liesl. I've dreamed of playing Liesl for years. How could Sara have that part? Trevor and I had it all planned out.

The part of the Mother Abbess went to a senior. Thank goodness. At least I didn't have to worry about that.

But what part was I going to get? What was left? Oh, there was the part of Elsa, the baroness. That might not be a bad role. I would get to dress elegantly, and there was at least one good song, maybe two. No dancing. Hmm…maybe some dancing in the ballroom scene. Not as good as the gazebo, but I guess it would have to do.

But wait, wasn't Elsa supposed to be in love with the Captain? They didn't have to kiss, did they? Because if Jake was playing the Captain, I wouldn't want to be playing someone in love with him. Too weird.

"Max Detweiller will be played by Jake Landon."

Jake wasn't going to be the Captain.

"Elsa will be played by Lauren Gardner."

"That's great," I said quickly, leaning past Trevor, "you get to be on stage with Jake a lot." Because, after all, that was her goal.

Lauren nodded, looking a little like I must have looked when I found out that I didn't have Liesl. She was really hoping to be Maria. So, who would play Maria?

On stage, Mrs. Valente was continuing, "The part of Captain von Trapp will be played by Mike Anderson, and the part of Maria will be played by Emma Landon."

This time I didn't shout out.

I was too stunned.

I had the role of Maria.
I had the lead in the play.
The lead.
I was going to be Maria in *The Sound of Music*.

Chapter 3
"Doorbells and Sleigh Bells and Schnitzel with Noodles"

"Emma, you got the lead!" Caitlyn shouted above the noise in the auditorium.

Excited chatter floated all around us as people got ready to leave, talking about the parts they had and the parts they wish they'd gotten. But, it was all a dull roar to me, as if I were underwater or in a far off room.

I had the lead.

Trevor put his arm around me and pulled me close for a hug. "That's great, Em," he said, "though now I can't sing to you."

I didn't get the part of Liesl. I got the lead.

Jake came over from where he had been sitting and gave me a little punch in the shoulder. "Awesome. Good thing for you I'm not playing the Captain."

I was going to be Maria.

The part Lauren had dreamed of.

My heart sank. I looked over at Lauren. She wasn't looking at me as she put her coat on, getting ready to go home. She had the same expression on her face as she did after she didn't make the National Honor Society: like she was trying not to cry.

I didn't want her to be sad. I wanted her to be happy. She had a good part. I had a better part, true. But I wanted her to be happy for me. And I wanted her to be happy for herself. "Elsa is a great role," I said.

She looked over at me, and she looked so sad I

just wanted to put my arms around her and tell her I was sorry. But what was I sorry for? That I got the best role? I couldn't really be sorry about that.

"Yeah"—she swallowed hard—"and you'll make a great Maria." She turned away quickly and didn't hear me say thank you. I don't think she wanted to hear.

"I have to go catch the late bus." Trevor moved his arm from around me and put on his coat.

I nodded and turned my attention back to Lauren. "You and Jake share a bunch of scenes," I said to her back. I needed to make this better somehow.

She barely turned toward me as she said, "Not as many as you and Mike."

Mike.

Biker Mike had the role of the Captain.

He had practically transformed into the Captain at auditions yesterday. I looked over to where he was putting on his leather jacket and gathering his things. He totally didn't look like a staid and courtly sea captain. Trevor looked more like he belonged in the part—he at least looked respectable. If Trevor had the part of the Captain, that would be awesome. Very romantic.

Caitlyn edged past me. "So awesome, Em. Congrats."

"And you as a nun!" I laughed.

She laughed too. "It will take all my acting abilities to pull that off. You think you have the hardest role as the lead. Don't be fooled. I have the hardest!" She gave Trevor a nudge. "Come on, the late bus will be going soon."

Trevor stood. "Right." He turned to me. "I'll pick you up tonight at seven?"

I stood too. "Sounds good. And I knew you'd get the part of Rolf." I smiled at him.

"Of course it won't be the same without you playing Liesl," he said.

True. So true. "But Sara will be great in the role." I looked around for her. She hadn't said anything to me after the roles were announced. I spotted her waiting by the back door for me and Jake so she could go home.

"One sister is very much like another?" Trevor asked.

"As if!" We looked alike—at least we both had the same light-colored hair and a smattering of freckles—but that was about it. Sara was the anti-Emma. Everything I liked she hated. I loved to dance, she preferred jogging or soccer; I loved being on stage, she wanted to fade into the background; I loved fashionable clothes, she was content to wear jeans and a T-shirt day after day. Maybe getting the role of Liesl would make her like being on stage and we'd actually have something in common.

"I can come over to your house and work on lines with her," Trevor suggested.

My heart gave a lurch: romances could start during plays. I knew that well enough.

But Trevor winked at me. "That would mean a lot of time at your house."

"It would, wouldn't it?" I kissed him on the cheek. "Bonus."

And then he and Caitlyn left to catch the late bus.

Caitlyn blew a kiss over her shoulder. "Cheers," she said as she bounced up the aisle.

"You ready?" Jake asked, looking bored as he leaned against a seat in the row in front of me.

I put on my coat. "Yeah." I looked over at Lauren again. She still looked like she wanted to cry. I wish I could make this better. "You're giving Lauren a ride home too, right?" I asked. That was the routine. When it was cold and nasty Jake drove us home. When it was nice, we walked. Lauren only lived around the block from us.

"Naturally." He looked at Lauren too, and his

eyes lost their teasing look and became soft and gentle. "Baroness, your carriage awaits," he said and held out an arm.

Lauren looked up, surprise in her eyes, a little bit of a smile escaping. "Why, thank you, Max, you old rogue."

I sighed. Things were okay. Lauren was flirting with Jake. She wouldn't still be upset I got her part now. But as we climbed into the Subaru wagon—and Jake insisted that Lauren take the front seat instead of sitting in back with me—Lauren didn't turn to me and talk to me or anything. Usually we talked nonstop the whole ride home.

What could I say? I'd already told her she would make a great Elsa. I wasn't going to apologize that I got the lead, because that wouldn't be honest. I was sorry Lauren was upset, but I was not sorry I got the role of Maria.

"It sure is cold out," was the lame comment I managed to come up with.

No one bothered to answer me. It didn't really warrant an answer.

Jake pulled into our driveway. "Out, you two. I'm going to take Lauren home."

"See you later," I said trying to keep my voice upbeat and normal, before I shut my door.

"Yeah," Lauren mumbled, not looking at me.

Sara and I walked up to the house. It had been so cold lately that no one had wanted to go out and bring in the Christmas decorations. I was getting kind of tired of seeing the robotic reindeer in the front yard. Sara didn't say anything as I unlocked the door. She just stormed past me once it was open, up to her room. And what exactly was her problem?

I spun around in a circle hugging myself. I had the lead—the actual lead in the school play. I stopped spinning and sat on the sofa. It was no fun to celebrate alone. But Lauren was jealous, and Sara had an attitude. It wasn't fair.

The phone in the kitchen rang and I hurried to answer it. Maybe it was Lauren. Maybe she was calling to tell me she really was happy for me. I grabbed the phone before it went to voice mail. The voice on the other end was male. Definitely not Lauren. But of course Lauren would call me on my cell phone, not the house phone, and she probably wasn't even home yet.

"Emma?" the voice on the phone said.

The voice was familiar, but I couldn't place it.

"This is Mike."

Mike? Biker Mike? I sat down at the breakfast counter and picked an apple out of the fruit bowl.

"I just wanted to tell you congratulations on getting the lead."

How did he get my number? I rolled the apple back and forth in front of me. Of course, it's not like our number is unlisted.

"Thanks. Same to you. I didn't know you were such an actor."

"I am a man of surprising depths," he said.

He was? I put the apple back in the bowl.

"We should get together to go over lines and stuff."

Get together with Biker Mike? Not my idea of a good time. "I don't know. I'm kind of busy."

"And about to be busier with the lead in the play."

I laughed. "I suppose that's true, isn't it."

"Anyway. We don't have to go over lines tonight or anything. But…whenever."

"Maybe." Going over lines outside of rehearsal was really helpful. It probably wouldn't be a bad idea—if it were anyone but Biker Mike.

"Yeah, so, I just wanted to congratulate you, you know," Mike said.

"You too." There was an awkward pause. "I'll see you at rehearsals," I said finally.

"Right. Monday after school. I'm looking forward

to it."

I hung up the phone. Weird. But kind of nice. I probably should have said something to him when we were still in the auditorium.

Up in my room I threw my book bag on my bed and stripped off my uniform skirt and blouse and slipped into comfy jeans and a sweatshirt that had been patiently waiting for me in a pile by my bed. My mother was always after me to clean my room. But my method of organization worked just fine. I took out my script, so I could start reading through my part.

There was a tentative knock at my door. Sara. Even her knock sounded unsure of itself. "Come in," I called.

Sara walked in and sat on my bed. Her social skills really needed improving. I sat in my saucer chair. "So, what do you want?" I finally asked.

"You told me I wouldn't have to say anything," Sara said suddenly. "*Probably a part without any lines at all*," she said in mocking sing-song voice. "That's what you said. '*My freshman year I had no lines. No worries*.'" She looked at me, her eyes narrowed to slits. "And look what happened. I have one of the main parts! What am I going to do?"

"I forgot to congratulate you, Sara. It is so awesome that you got that role. It's a fantastic part!"

"I don't want it!" Sara protested. "So what do I do now?"

I ran my finger along one of the seams on the chair. "I guess you practice the part and knock them dead out there on opening night and get ready for a great career in theater."

"Emma!" Sara shouted, frustration filling her voice. "You are not listening to me."

"I am." Here I was, not doing anything else, what else could I be doing but listening to her?

"You promised me I wouldn't have a big part." She glared at me, locking eyes with me until I looked away first. You would think I had tortured her kitten or something.

"It's not like I assigned the parts, Sara." I met her gaze again. "Mrs. Valente must have been really impressed with your audition. Be glad."

"I'm not *glad*, I'm mad. I never would have gone to callbacks if I thought I'd actually have to sing a solo." She stood up and paced around the room, stopping to pick up my hairbrush and brandish it at me like some sort of a weapon. "A solo! Do you believe that?"

Of course I believed it. I'd been practicing *her* solo for the past couple of weeks, hoping to have that very part. "This is a good thing, Sara. Really it is. There's no reason to be worried about it. Mrs. Valente wouldn't have given you the part if she didn't think you could do it."

"She probably just wanted to give you both parts, but couldn't figure out a way to clone you. Won't she be surprised when she finds out that I'm not at all like you," Sara muttered.

"Maybe you're more like me than you thought," I said. "And I'm sure Mrs. Valente gave you the part based on your own merits—not because of me or Jake."

She flopped back onto the bed, still holding the hairbrush. "Will you help?" she asked, sounding scared and uncertain.

"Sure," I answered. "There's no reason to be nervous."

Sara sat up. "No reason? There's plenty of reasons. I have a solo to sing. Well, a duet really, with Trevor. But part of it is just me. What if I forget the words or lose my place or something? I'll mess everything up and everyone will laugh."

"That won't happen," I said. "There will be lots of practicing—to the point where you'll be able to do it in your sleep."

"More like a nightmare," Sara muttered, then

she turned to me and pointed the hairbrush at me again. "Aren't you nervous?"

"No." I'd never had such a big role before. Maybe I should be nervous.

"Have you even looked at the script?" She pointed to the script in my hand. "You have more lines than anyone. You have more songs than anyone. I'm sure glad it's not me that has that part."

She didn't even want the part she had. But Mrs. Valente must have thought I could handle the lead, otherwise she wouldn't have given me the role, just like Sara could be Liesl. "I can do it. And so can you," I assured her.

Sara shrugged and ran her fingers over the design on my quilt. "At least I like the song 'Sixteen Going on Seventeen.' And I get to sing it with Trevor. He's sweet. I guess that will be all right."

That's right. Sara would be living my romantic fantasy with Trevor. She would get to dance the gazebo scene, except there was no leaping around the benches dance. She would have him sing dreamily into her eyes. I frowned. "Don't forget he's my boyfriend."

"Oh, for Pete's sake. I'm not going after your boyfriend." Sara jumped up from the bed, and threw the hairbrush down. "I'm not a little you. I don't need your boyfriend. I can get my own."

"Sorry." I held my hands up in surrender. Time for a change of topic. "Are you going out tonight?"

"Of course. I'm not a total loser. Shelly and I are going to the mall to hang out."

Since Sara was obviously planning on being insulted by anything I said, I needed a peace offering. "If you want to borrow any of my clothes, you can," I offered.

Sara gave me a withering glare. "Why would I want to borrow your clothes? Am I not stylish enough for you? Are jeans not 'in' enough for you? Should I use your hair iron before I go too?"

"It was just a suggestion."

"Well, stop suggesting things to me," she said, her hands on her hips.

"You're the one who came into my room," I retorted.

"Not to have a makeover of my personality."

I was going to lose it soon. "All I said was you could borrow some of my clothes. What's so loathsome about that? I was being nice. Some sisters wouldn't let you touch their clothes."

"Yeah, aren't I lucky that I have Miss Perfect Emma for my big sister?"

"I'm not perfect," I said trying very hard not to yell.

"And don't you forget it," she snapped, as she sailed out of my room.

I picked up a stuffed animal—as I wished I could pick up my sister—and threw it across the room.

What would "Maria" do to make herself feel better?

She'd sing "My Favorite Things."

I turned my CD player on—*The Sound of Music* CD was already in it—and put it straight on that song. "*Raindrops on roses and whiskers on kittens,*" I sang along. I was feeling better already. "*When the dog bites, when the bee stings,*" I belted out, "*when I'm feeling—*"

The door opened, and I stopped in my tracks, to face my father. He smiled at me.

"I knocked, but you must not have heard," he said.

I turned down the music. "I got the lead, Dad!" I nearly shouted, flinging myself at him. "I'm Maria!"

"I know." He gave me a hug and then sat on my bed. "Sara told me when I came in. Congratulations. I'm not surprised. You always were my little 'drama queen'."

I wrinkled my nose and sat down on the bed

next to him. "Not funny," I said.

He put one arm around my shoulders and gave me a squeeze. "I'm very proud. I know you'll be great."

"Thanks. Sara's Liesl. And Jake is Max."

"How did I end up with such talented kids?"

"Recessive genes," I answered. Our father was an accountant. He couldn't even sing "Happy Birthday" on key.

"That must be it," he laughed.

At least he was comfortable with his lack of talent.

"Your mother won't be home for dinner tonight," Dad said. "She has to work late. I'm going to order a pizza. That okay with you?"

Certainly better than eating my father's cooking.

He left and I lay on my bed and stared at the ceiling. I needed to talk to Lauren. I didn't know what I was going to say, but she was my best friend. We couldn't let years of best-frienddom be ruined by me getting the part she wanted in a play. If our friendship had survived the lunchbox incident of second grade, and the very unfortunate "but I liked Matt first" incident of sixth grade, we surely could survive this.

We just needed to talk.

I picked up my phone and called her. She didn't answer. I left a text message, but she didn't respond. I turned on my computer. I could IM her. But she wasn't online either. I didn't want to just leave her a message. We needed to actually talk to each other.

I called Caitlyn. "Hey 'Sister' Cait."

Caitlyn laughed. "All kinds of dead nuns are turning over in their graves at that one."

"Have you talked to Lauren?" I asked, almost afraid to know the answer.

"Yeah." Caitlyn snapped her gum into the phone, which was sort of annoying. "She's pretty bummed that she didn't get Maria."

"She got a really good role."

"Yeah. But you got Maria. She had dreams, you know."

"I know." I sighed. "It's not my fault."

"Doesn't change how she feels." I could hear Caitlyn chewing her gum. "Just give her time, Em. You two have been friends since you were in preschool, it's not going to end over this."

I really hoped she was right.

At seven o'clock Trevor's mom pulled into the driveway. Sixteen in New Jersey meant the indignity of having a parent escort you on your dates. His mom dropped us off at the mall movie theater and promised to pick us up in the same spot at ten sharp.

Once she was out of sight, Trevor took hold of my hand. "I thought we'd see *Freakazoid*, how's that sound?"

It didn't sound like my ideal movie, that was for sure. But Trevor and I had a deal: I went to wacky adventure movies with him and he went to school dances with me.

As we ate our popcorn and waited for the previews to start, Trevor said, "I'll have to sing 'Sixteen Going on Seventeen' to Sara now."

I stopped, my hand halfway to the popcorn. "But that's our song." I loved the way he would sing that song to me when we were walking to class and stuff. It was so cute.

"But you're not going to be Liesl."

"Well, yeah. So on stage you'll sing it to her. You can still sing it to me off stage. I'm still sixteen going on seventeen, after all."

He shrugged and took another handful of popcorn. I watched him eat it, waiting for him to say something else. Finally, when the last kernel in his hand was gone, and he'd wiped his palm on his jeans, he turned to me and said, "I don't know. It wouldn't seem right."

"You'll have to find something else to sing to me, then." I put my hand on his jean-covered knee. "In fact, Sara got a Karaoke machine for Christmas. You can use that to sing to me." I could actually picture Trevor doing that too.

He put his hand over mine. "It's not quite the same."

"Not quite. But still fun." I leaned forward and gave him a quick kiss.

"It's too bad that hoodlum got the part of the Captain."

I didn't say anything. Mike did kind of look like a hoodlum, but in every encounter I'd had with him so far he'd been pretty nice.

"And I hate the fact that you're going to be 'married' to him in the play."

"It's just acting," I assured.

"I just hope he doesn't ruin the play."

"He won't. You saw him try out. He was awesome."

"I didn't notice. I only had eyes for you," Trevor said and put his arm around me as the lights went down and the previews started.

Chapter 4
"Let's Start at the Very Beginning"

When my alarm clock went off on Monday morning, I didn't hit snooze like I usually did. I opened my eyes and grinned. Today was the day we started rehearsals. I couldn't wait.

The sun was just starting to come up when I got down to the kitchen. Mom was already there, looking immaculate in her blue Dior suit. She was adjusting her pearl earrings while waiting for the coffee to finish.

I poured myself a glass of orange juice and sat down at my usual spot at the breakfast bar, across from Sara.

"You have to have more than that in your stomach, Emma," my mother chastised. I knew the lecture. It was mother lecture number four: A good breakfast is the cornerstone to a good day.

I was too excited to eat, but in order to be spared further lectures, I poured a handful of cornflakes in a bowl and added a splash of milk. Jake came in, and without a word to anyone, started concocting some sort of an egg and sausage sandwich. Nothing ever affected his appetite. Sara was picking raisins out of a cinnamon raisin bagel.

"Rehearsals are right after school?" Mom asked, as she sat down with a cup of coffee. All she ever has for breakfast is coffee, but I certainly wasn't going to point out the hypocrisy in that.

Jake nodded and flipped his egg over.

Sara groaned.

I answered, "Yes. We'll probably bc about two hours later than normal."

"That's good. With tax season getting under way, your father will be home later and later—it's less time for you to spend alone in the house."

"Will you be home by the time we get back?" Sara asked.

"Probably not. But I shouldn't be too late tonight. There's a lasagna in the fridge. The first one home, please put it in the oven."

Jake promised it would be done. And since lasagna was his favorite food, I was pretty sure he wouldn't forget.

"I wish you hadn't gotten me into this whole stupid play thing," Sara said to me, looking up from dissecting her bagel.

"Yeah, Em," Jake said, sitting down next to me, his completed sandwich on a plate. "How dare you encourage her to do something that lands her a great honor, like a major role in a school play." He winked at me, but it wasn't enough to diffuse my annoyance at Sara.

Sara stuck her tongue out at him.

"Enough already," I snapped, pounding the table so hard that one of my corn flakes leaped out of the bowl. "You auditioned. You got a good role. Be glad."

"Don't give up on it before you've even gone to the first rehearsal." Mom offered her calming words of wisdom, peering at us from over her coffee cup.

"Fine," Sara said through clenched teeth. "I'll give it a chance." She looked right at me. "But, I'm not going to like it. You don't like playing soccer, so why should I like something you like?"

The phone rang and I jumped for it, glad for an excuse not to have to answer Sara. Maybe it was Lauren. Maybe she was finally returning my calls. I'd waited all weekend. I checked the caller ID as I scooped up the phone. It was Lauren. Yay!

"Hi Lauren," I said cheerily. If I just acted as if nothing had been wrong between us then it could be true, right?

"Hi." Lauren's voice sounded odd and tight. "I just wanted Jake to know he doesn't have to pick me up for school today. My Mom's driving me."

It felt like a lead ball had just dropped to the bottom of my stomach. "Oh. Yeah, I'll tell him." I could salvage this. "Did you have a good weekend?"

"It was okay."

"Are you excited about rehearsals today?"

"Listen, Em, I've gotta go. Just tell Jake I don't need a ride. Thanks." And then she hung up.

I gently replaced the phone and swallowed hard before turning to face my watching family, my face burning. "Lauren doesn't need a ride today," I said to Jake while staring into my cereal bowl. The cornflakes left in there had all the appeal of soggy cardboard right now.

Lauren just needed a little bit of time. That's all it was. She would talk to me when she was ready. Maybe by lunchtime.

****

At lunchtime my locker opened on the first try, proof that things were starting to go my way. I was ready and waiting when Trevor and Caitlyn got there. Lauren wasn't with them. Their lockers are near each other, so they usually showed up together.

"Where's Lauren?" I looked over Trevor's shoulder to see if maybe she was coming down the hallway.

"I think she's talking to one of her teachers," Caitlyn said.

Trevor just put his arm around me as we were engulfed in the noisy crowd heading to the cafeteria, from where the smells of ziti, or some tomato-sauce based food, wafted. We found our usual spot, but Lauren wasn't there. I took out my peanut butter and jelly sandwich, but no one bothered to make fun of it. Where could Lauren be?

And then I spotted her across the room, talking and laughing with some other girls in our class. She wasn't sitting with us? Lauren and I had eaten lunch together every day since first grade. Was she really that jealous that she wouldn't even sit with me at lunch? My eyes burned with tears I was not going to shed. I blinked a few times and took a deep breath. I wanted to have the lead, but I also wanted Lauren to still be my best friend. Couldn't I have both?

Caitlyn looked where I was looking and sighed. Then she pasted on a bright smile. "You'll never guess what I found on YouTube last night. There was this old TV show about this wacky nun who could fly. *The Flying Nun*. How weird is that? Do you think if I got a big enough hat like she had—and trust me she had a wild big hat—I could fly? Maybe they could rig up some wires in the theater like they did for *Peter Pan* and stuff. A big hat, some pixie dust or whatever, and I could fly away. It would make an interesting addition to the show, don't you think?"

"Why don't you suggest that to Mrs. Valente," Trevor said.

I didn't say anything. I just kept staring at Lauren, sitting on the other side of the cafeteria, her back to me.

When I got to the auditorium after classes, Lauren and Caitlyn were already sitting in the front row. Figuring I wasn't going to go where I wasn't wanted, I led Trevor to seats a few rows back. As I sat staring at the gum stuck to the back of the seat in front of me, wondering how I was going to survive life without my best friend, Sara came in with Jake. They sat down next to me.

"I don't know how you let me get into this," Sara muttered.

I scrunched up my nose. "Stop complaining. It's getting old already."

Mrs. Valente stood on the stage. "I want to just do a read through of the play today—no singing, no acting things out—just a read through. Let's have the nuns—that includes the Mother Abbess and Maria—up on stage. Sit on the edge of the stage here and you'll read your parts."

The girl who was playing Sister Sophia raised her hand. "Um, Mrs. Valente, what are these words?" she asked, looking at the first page of her script.

"That's Latin, Sami. Don't worry, you won't be asked to translate it, only to sing it."

We went through scene five. Then the nuns all got off the stage and were replaced by the Captain, Franz, and Frau Schmidt (the butler and housekeeper), and the children; I stayed where I was on the edge of the stage.

Mike climbed up and sat next to me. I could smell his aftershave. A quick look told me he'd shaved since the other day, too. Trevor sometimes put on aftershave before we went out, but he only had to shave maybe once a month.

Mike sat so close to me that I could feel the warmth of his body next to mine. My skin tingled. What would it be like if he held my hand? Would his hand be calloused or smooth? Dry or sweaty? I shook my head to clear it. I had to concentrate on reading my part.

"Is Maria nervous?" Mike said under his breath.

"Not at all," I responded.

"Mike, that's your line," Mrs. Valente said.

"Oh, sorry…" Mike quickly found his spot.

And he was asking if I was nervous!

We went through the whole play. I was in almost every scene—at least to some extent. This play was going to be a lot of work.

"Tomorrow," Mrs. Valente said, "we'll start blocking out some of the scenes, and work on some of the songs. Start memorizing your lines."

****

The next day at rehearsal I sat in the front row

between Trevor and Sara. Lauren had sat at a different table at lunch again, and in a different row in the auditorium. So, fine. If she didn't want to talk to me, I wouldn't talk to her.

At least at rehearsals Trevor and I would get to spend time together—even if I didn't have the role of Liesl. But then Mrs. Valente sent him away. Of course, not just him. Everyone who was not a nun was sent into the gym to work on some of the other songs and dance steps. The only people left in the auditorium were me and a bunch of girls playing nuns. At least Caitlyn was with me. But this was not what I envisioned when I wanted to be in the play with my friends and boyfriend!

It seemed to take forever to teach the "nuns" how to pronounce the Latin words in their opening song. Sami, as Sister Sophia, was the worst, deciding that since the words looked kind of like Italian she should pronounce them as if she were in *The Godfather* or something. I tried to ignore them as I sat by myself in the first row and read over the words to my song, "The Sound of Music."

The nuns finished. Caitlyn came down and plopped herself next to me. "Whoever thought having a part with no speaking lines would be so hard! Yikes. But now I can go home and tell my dad I've been learning Latin. He'll be so pleased. He thinks it should be mandatory in Catholic schools or something."

And then it was my turn to get on stage. I wouldn't need help pronouncing my words: they were in English. I even knew the whole song by heart. We should be moving on to the next scene in just a couple of minutes.

Ha.

First I didn't sit right. How is there a wrong way to sit on the floor?

Then once we got that part settled, Mrs. Valente kept stopping me every couple of lines to tell me to move to another part of the stage. The whole process took forever.

We went through the scene three times before Mrs. Valente moved us on to the next scene. I got back down from the stage, while the nuns went back up to sing "Maria." Once again, I was alone in the audience.

I knew it was lonely at the top, but I thought that was meant figuratively.

I studied my lines while Mrs. Valente and the nuns went through the same painful process I just had with my song.

The more I read of the script, the more I liked the part of Maria. She loved to sing. And sometimes life threw her a curve ball. In her case, she had to leave the convent. In my case, I got the lead role instead of the one I'd been dreaming of. And in her case, everything worked out just fine. Would that be true for me too?

On stage, the nuns had gotten to the end of their song, and Mrs. Valente had them start again from the beginning.

It was going to be a long day.

Finally, I got to go on stage, and, script in hand, I had my first on-stage dialogue with Mother Abbess. And then it was back to more painful blocking of songs while trying to sing them. At least we should only have to do this process once for each song.

Hopefully.

Finally, we finished those first few songs. Now Mrs. Valente would have to call in the rest of the cast so we could move on. Now I would get to see Trevor again.

But no. Now we started from the beginning again.

Sigh.

For two hours we worked on those first four scenes of the play. At last we were done, and the exiles came back in to collect their belongings. They came in laughing and joking. Apparently a great time was had by all in the gym.

Jake's friend Justin was there too. He was stage manager this year and had been building scenes in the art room. "How about a little Snack Shack?" he said, wiping paint spattered hands on the pair of old jeans he was wearing. It had been our after rehearsal routine last year.

"Sounds good," I answered. Lauren would have to speak to me if we were sitting at the same table, sharing nachos at the Snack Shack. Things would get back to normal.

"Sure," Trevor said. "If you can give me a ride home after."

"Me too." Caitlyn whipped out her phone. "But if I'm going to miss the late bus, I need to call my mom. How will I get home?" she asked before dialing.

Justin smiled, "I'll give you a ride, Miss Cait."

She grinned. "Well then. Sounds like a plan."

But Lauren just buttoned up her coat. "I'd rather go home."

Fine. I swallowed over the lump in my throat and put on my jacket.

Jake looked around at the rest of us and shrugged. "I guess I can take her home and meet the rest of you there."

Jake and Lauren started to leave the auditorium.

"You're being a real jerk, you know," Caitlyn said, at my elbow.

"Me? She's the one not talking to me," I protested.

"Seems to me like you're not talking to each other," Caitlyn said and started to walk out of the auditorium.

Darn. But Lauren started it. Maybe I could end it. If I tried. I took a deep breath, grabbed my backpack, and headed up the aisle after them. “Lauren, wait,” I called out.

She stopped and turned, although her face was a mask. I stood in front of her. She was waiting for me to say something. *I* was waiting for me to say something. But what?

“Please go to the Snack Shack. You’re the only one who knows just the right number of creamers to pour in the hot chocolate to make it perfect.” It was lame. Really lame.

But Lauren shrugged. “I guess.”

It wasn’t exactly détente, but it was a start.

I smelled a familiar aftershave. I turned around and there was Mike. My heart beat a little faster as I looked at that too-long hair and the closed-off expression. Maybe it was time someone included him in stuff around here. “Want to go to the Snack Shack with us?” I asked.

His eyes widened slightly and he gave me a half smile. “That’s like the ‘in’ place?”

“The in-est.” I said.

He raised his eyebrows at my made-up word. Then he shrugged and said, “I guess I’ll check it out.”

“Good.” I smiled at him.

He winked at me and the heat rose in my face. I looked down so he wouldn’t see me blush.

Trevor put his arm around me, steering me away from Mike. When I looked up at him he was frowning. “Why’d you invite him?” he asked, leading me out to Jake’s car.

“And who exactly is he going to ride with?” Jake added as he joined us. Justin was driving Caitlin in his pickup truck and the rest of us were squeezing into the Subaru.

Mike headed to his motorcycle parked at the end of the parking lot. “He’s self sufficient, he’ll drive himself,” I said to Jake. Though who drives a motorcycle in ten degree weather? He must be nuts.

"And," I gave my attention to Trevor, "he's in the play with us. We should include him."

"He creeps me out," Sara said as we climbed into the car.

"You don't know him," I answered. I slid into the middle so Trevor could squeeze in.

"And you do?" Sara countered.

"No. But none of us know him. Maybe we should give him a chance."

Trevor put his hand on my knee. "You're like a little Mother Teresa looking out for the underdog," he said, his tone snarky. "How sweet."

The Snack Shack was only a couple of blocks from St. Stephen's High School, which was why it was the most popular hang out. Mike got there first and snagged one of the retro pink and green booths just as another group left. We all slid in.

"Today is total hot chocolate weather," I said.

"They should put a Starbucks near school. Then we could get coffee," Caitlyn said, bouncing a little in her seat.

"Ha, like you of all people need the caffeine," Jake said.

"You can get coffee here," Mike answered, quite reasonably, but he didn't know Caitlyn that well.

"Yeah, but not Starbucks coffee."

"Well, good old Snack Shack hot chocolate is good enough for me," I said.

"It's probably from a powder mix or something," Sara said.

I was surrounded by negativity. I threw a packet of sugar at her. "Who cares? It's *hot*!"

Naturally, when the waitress came around everyone ordered hot chocolate, and Justin insisted on a double order of nachos for the table.

"Emma, you should have heard Lauren, Jake, and Mike singing 'No Way to Stop It.' They were phenomenal," Sara said as we waited for the drinks and food.

"I wish I could have. I was busy listening to a bunch of girls mangle Latin."

"Hey," Caitlyn protested, wrinkling her nose and tossing a sugar packet at me. "It's not like we've ever heard those crazy words before."

"How do you know they were mangling it?" Trevor touched my nose in a teasing way. "You don't know Latin."

"That's true." I started to explain how Mrs. Valente kept correcting them, but Mike interrupted.

"*Quid est veritas?*"

"What?"

Mike shrugged and slowly ripped a napkin in half, the edge of a tattoo peeking out from behind the sleeve of his leather jacket. "What is truth? I had to take Latin at my old school."

He knew Latin? There was definitely more to Mike than I ever would have imagined.

"I'm surprised he's mastered English," Trevor muttered.

I gave his leg a shove. What if Mike had heard him?

"That's rough, man," Jake said. "I'm glad they don't make us take Latin at St. Stephen's."

The food arrived and we all dug in.

"Sara blew me away singing 'Sixteen Going on Seventeen'," Jake said as he dipped a nacho in cheese. "Mrs. Valente certainly picked the right person for that part."

My chin went up. That was supposed to be my part. Sara shouldn't be better at it than I would have been. But it was silly to be jealous. After all, I had the lead. I had to be happy for Sara. Even if she was singing a romantic song with my boyfriend.

"And you were nervous," I said as I took a nacho from the plate.

Sara shrugged. "Perfectly normal to be nervous." Then she grinned wickedly. "There are some pretty funny people in this school. You should have seen

Miss Davis try to teach dance steps. 'No no. Your other right foot!'"

Her imitation of the gym teacher was perfect. If Sara were simply allowed to mimic people all day, she'd have it made. I looked across the booth at Lauren who was silently pouring creamers into her hot chocolate. She hadn't said anything the whole time we were here.

"How many creamers is it again?" I asked her. "What's the magic number?"

"Three," Lauren said, but she didn't even look up as she said it.

I sighed. At least I'd tried. I told them what we'd accomplished in the theater and Mike said, "Scene five tomorrow?"

"That's what Mrs. Valente said." I blew on my hot chocolate to cool it down enough to drink.

"That's the scene where Maria and the Captain meet, isn't it?" Mike asked.

I looked up at him and his eyes grabbed mine and held until I shivered.

I pulled my eyes away from his piercing blue ones and stared into my hot chocolate. "I believe so," I answered.

"Scene six is Trevor's and my scene," Sara said. She looked up from her drink and smiled at Trevor.

"I can't wait to see it," I said, even though my stomach hurt at the thought of her doing the scene I'd been dreaming of.

****

At least the next afternoon, Trevor got to stay with me. Only the nuns, and Jake and Lauren, were sent out to work on other scenes in the gym. I happily sat next to Trevor in the auditorium, holding his hand. This was what I had in mind when I wanted to be in the play with my boyfriend: being together.

But we didn't get to be together for long. We started with scene five. And even though there were a couple of pages of dialogue before I made my appearance, Mrs.Valente wanted me backstage, ready and waiting.

The scene started with the Captain, blowing on his whistle to summon his help. Right away Mrs. Valente started giving Mike instructions about where to stand, where to walk to, what to do—and that was even before he had a line to say. At least I knew I wasn't the only one who had to go through this. Finally, the three people who started the scene were on stage: Mike, and "Franz," and "Frau Schmidt." Mrs. Valente let them get through their dialogue once before making them start over again, giving stage direction the whole time. I'd never get on stage at this rate. I could have been out there sitting next to Trevor this whole time, holding hands, whispering to each other. It would have been much more fun than standing back here just waiting. Would they ever get to my cue?

Sara was backstage with me, also waiting, with the other Von Trapp children, for her cue, which was shortly after mine.

"Do you think we'll ever get out there?" Sara asked.

I laughed. Great minds think alike.

I jumped when Sara stamped her foot. "Maybe I don't know as much about theater as you do," she said sharply, "but that doesn't mean you should laugh at me when I ask a simple question."

I tried to say something, to explain, but she walked away before I had a chance.

Finally, I got to go on stage. And I was on my own. Again, before I even said a word, Mrs. Valente stopped me.

"Emma, you will have a satchel and a guitar case with you. You will put them down, look around the room, exploring. When you hear the Abbey bells you will kneel and bow your head in prayer. When Mike comes in you will cross yourself, stand up, and turn to him."

"Right." I knew all that. I'd read the stage direction too. But at least it was vague enough that I could maybe interpret it my way, and since we didn't have any props or set yet, Mrs. Valente couldn't get too specific with her requests. I knelt in prayer, and then as per the stage directions, Mike came in. I crossed myself and stood up.

When I turned to face him, it was like the day of auditions. Something about the way he was standing, with his feet apart, his hands behind his back, a serious look on his face, made it seem as if he were actually the Captain.

I felt unaccountably flustered.

He said his first line. "*I'm Captain von Trapp. You are Fraulein…*"

I blinked. Who was I? I looked at the script. "*Maria,*" I said quickly, "*Maria Rainer.*"

I gained confidence as we exchanged a few more lines. I became the new governess meeting her intimidating boss for the first time. And then it was time for Maria to meet the children. They came on stage led by Sara. Since they had practiced part of this the day before, Mrs. Valente didn't have to stop too much with stage directions—until we got to the next song.

"Do Re Mi." A very fun song. A lot of people to position properly. And once we finally got it right, we had to do it again. And again. I was beginning to think we were never going to move on, when suddenly, we did.

"Okay. We have time for one more scene. Sara. Trevor. On stage. Let's do scene six."

Finally, I got to sit in the audience. I watched from the front row as Sara and Trevor read their lines and sang "Sixteen Going on Seventeen" together. As much as I loved the role of Maria, part of me still wanted to be Liesl. I should be up there having Trevor sing that song to me.

"*Liesl*, face more toward the audience when you sing," Mrs. Valente interrupted.

Sara did as she was told and continued.

"Sing a bit louder dear," Mrs. Valente interrupted again.

Sara started again, louder.

"You need to face toward *Rolf,* too. You are singing to him, after all."

"If you didn't think I could do this, then why did you give me the part?" Sara burst out and ran backstage.

I sighed. Mrs. Valente had been giving everyone stage directions. It's all that had been going on here all afternoon. Why did Sara have to take things so personally?

Trevor disappeared backstage and so did Mrs. Valente. Sara was my sister, maybe I should go back there too and try to talk some sense into her. Then again, she hadn't been too willing to listen to my advice lately, maybe it was better to leave well enough alone.

Someone came and sat in the seat next to me. I was surprised to look up and see Mike.

"That kid is a little sensitive," he commented.

Yeah. No kidding. But I didn't like other people pointing that out. "She's my sister," I said, scuffing one foot along the ground. "She's just nervous."

"She's going to have to get over it." He looked over at me and smiled. He had a gorgeous smile, even though his bottom teeth were a little crooked. "I thought that was the part you were going to get."

My cheeks got hot; I was sure they were turning red. I looked down so he wouldn't notice and shrugged. "Best laid plans…and all that," I said.

"I'm glad you're Maria," he said.

I couldn't help it; I smiled at that. "Me too."

"When do you want to get together and go over some lines?"

I stole a look at Biker Mike. He wasn't really the

kind of person I pictured myself hanging out with. Trevor certainly wouldn't like it if I started spending time with Mike. But it would be rude to say that I didn't want to. "I've got a boyfriend."

"What's that got to do with it?" Mike asked, an edge to his voice that hadn't been there before. "I don't want to date you. I want to rehearse with you."

"I just wanted you to know, is all." I could feel the heat rising in my cheeks again. I hated blushing.

"Oh, *I* know," Mike said, running his finger over some initials carved into the seat in front of him.

And what exactly did he mean by that? I was not the kind of person who went around always saying they had a boyfriend. Only, I kind of had just done that, hadn't I? I kicked the leg of the chair in front of me. There was no time to pursue it, though, because Trevor, Sara, and Mrs. Valente emerged from backstage and continued the scene as if nothing had happened. This time, Sara willingly accepted Mrs. Valente's directions. And after they went through the scene two times, Mrs. Valente released us for the day.

"I need cheesy fries," Sara said as we put on our coats.

"Snack Shack it is," said Jake. "But Justin isn't here today, how will we get Caitlyn there?"

"Caitlyn has to go home," Caitlyn said. "I've got a dentist appointment." She wrinkled her nose in disgust. "Catch you all later." She left to catch the late bus.

When Jake, Lauren, Trevor, Sara, and I got to the Snack Shack, Mike was already there, pulling two tables together since all the booths were occupied.

"What's he doing here again?" Trevor asked with ill-disguised contempt. "Can't we just hang out without that hoodlum?"

"He's not a hoodlum," I said, "and he's in the play with us. Why shouldn't he hang out with us after rehearsals? Besides, he got us a table"

Mike waved us over. I turned to the others. They were looking for a non-existent other table to sit at. "Come on," I said and headed over to the one Mike had for us. They followed. "Good thing you snagged the table, Mike. Thanks."

"No problem," Mike said.

We all sat down, but conversation didn't come. Lauren still wasn't talking to me, and Trevor apparently had nothing to say to Mike. And Sara was in her own little world.

What fun.

Finally, when we had hot chocolates and cheesy fries in front of us, Jake asked, "So how'd rehearsal in the big house go today?"

"Great"

"Horrible"

Sara and I answered at the same time.

"*Liesl* do this, *Liesl* do that," Sara mimicked Mrs. Valente. "Isn't she just supposed to let our creative spirit soar? How can we do anything with her micromanaging our every move? It's bogus."

"She's just doing her job," I said. "She's the director. She's directing."

Trevor put a reassuring hand on Sara's arm. "You were fine."

Just a little too intimate if you asked me. I noticed Mike watching me and looked away.

"It's just rough in the beginning, with Mrs. Valente interrupting every few seconds to give stage direction," I explained. It was hardly like Sara was the only one who had Mrs. Valente down her throat. After all, it took me about ten times to just sit the way Mrs. Valente liked in my first scene. Of course, no one but the "nuns" knew about that.

"You don't have to make excuses for me," Sara said hotly.

"Who's making excuses?" I asked.

"I couldn't take the pressure, so I ran off the

stage. I made a fool of myself."

"What pressure? It's the first week of rehearsal. Lighten up, Sara."

"You don't know what it's like," Sara insisted.

Didn't I? "In my first scene it took like five minutes just to sit the way Mrs. Valente liked."

"Do you think that even compares?" Sara asked.

"Apparently, you don't," I said. "But you're not the only one Mrs. Valente gives stage direction to."

Sara stood up. "I'm not hungry. I'm going home." She put her coat on and left.Trevor stood up and put his coat on too. "I'll go talk to her. I do the scene with her. Maybe I can say something. I don't know." He threw a couple of dollars on the table and he left too.

And I watched him go.

"Close your mouth, Em, you look like a codfish," Jake said.

I clamped my mouth shut. But my boyfriend had just gone running after my sister. I had to do something. I stood up and put my coat on.

"I'm going after them," I said.

"Don't, Em," Lauren said in a warning tone.

"I have to," I said and left without looking back.

Chapter 5
"Fellows Will Fall in Line"

The frigid air sliced through me like a knife as I left the diner. I looked down the street. Sara and Trevor were already a block ahead of me, walking together and about to turn the corner. If I ran, perhaps I could catch up with them.

"Where are you going?"

I turned, surprised to find Mike standing behind me.

That was a stupid question. "Home," I called over my shoulder as I started walking. It was wicked cold out here. My knees, unprotected by my short skirt and knee socks, were freezing. On the upside, soon they'd be numb and I wouldn't mind anymore. I'd only gotten to the first cross street when I heard the revving of a motorcycle behind me. Mike pulled over next to me.

"Get on," he yelled over the sound of the engine.

I turned to him. "On your motorcycle?" Was he crazy? "No thanks. I don't have a death wish." The thing looked ancient, a rusty bucket of bolts. Was it even roadworthy?

"It's not dangerous."

Right. And I have beachfront property in Arizona to sell you. "No." I was not getting on a motorcycle. Not with Biker Mike or anyone else.

"Seriously, it's cold out here. You'll freeze to death."

"I don't think I'll freeze to death in ten minutes." I crossed the street and continued on my way. It *was* really cold out here. This was going to be a long ten minutes. Would it be possible to freeze to death in ten minutes?

Mike was waiting for me at the next corner. "Get on."

"I'm not riding on a motorcycle." I stamped my feet in an attempt to get some feeling back in to them.

He cut the engine on his bike so we didn't have to shout at each other.

"Why are you going home?" he asked.

"What do you mean, why? Trevor's on his way there with my sister." I turned to go.

"Don't you trust them?" Mike asked.

I turned to Mike and saw him looking at me with a direct and steady gaze, waiting for an answer. I stopped myself before I said no. If I didn't trust my boyfriend then we didn't really have much of a relationship now, did we?

"Of course I do," I said with as much disdain as I could.

"If you show up there right away, it's going to look like you can't even trust them to spend some time alone. Is that the impression you want to give your *boyfriend*?"

Of course it wasn't. And how dare Mike figure that out when I didn't see it. "What do you suggest I do instead?"

"Come home with me," Mike said it as if it were the most logical and normal idea in the world.

"Why would I do that?" I crossed my arms, partly to keep warm, and partly to let him know that I thought this was a silly idea and I would need some convincing.

"We can go over lines. You can give Sara a chance to calm down." He paused before continuing, "You can get warm."

Unfortunately his offer made sense. I wavered. It was really cold out, and I didn't want Trevor to think I didn't trust him. I looked uncertainly at the motorcycle. It looked like a bicycle on steroids. The red paint was splotchy and the handlebars reminded me of the ones on my first bike. The seat didn't even look like a motorcycle seat. It was more like a big bicycle seat. Would we both even fit on it?

Mike put down the kickstand and got off. "It's a 1941 Indian Chief. War surplus. Isn't it great? My Dad helps me fix it up when it's his weekend. We need to work on the paint next, but it runs like a dream."

I didn't know anything about motorcycles. "Yeah, it's nice, I guess."

He held out his helmet to me. The helmet was at least modern-looking, full around the head coverage, with flames painted on the sides.

"Don't you need this?" I hesitated before taking it from him.

"I'll take my chances, it's only a mile."

I didn't want to take chances. I still wasn't sure I wanted to be on the motorcycle at all, but at least I would wear the helmet. And keep my eyes closed.

Against all my better instincts, I put the helmet on. It was too big and felt strange on my head.

Mike climbed onto the bike. "Just climb on behind me."

Easier said than done. First of all, the seat did not look like it would hold both of us. And then there was the matter of my skirt. The St. Stephen's uniform skirt was never meant for motorcycle riding. I put one hand on Mike's shoulder and, using my other hand to keep my skirt from flying around, I swung my leg around the back of the bike and squeezed onto the seat behind Mike. Then with a bunch of fidgeting, I did my best to tuck my skirt under my legs. I could just imagine my skirt blowing up around me as we rode down the street—not a happy thought.

"Hold on tight," Mike called back to me.

It was kind of hard to hear with the helmet on. I grabbed him around the waist and held on tight. I didn't have much choice. There really wasn't room on that seat for the two of us. I was pressed so close to him I could feel his heart beating through both of our jackets. Or was that mine?

He started the bike up and I closed my eyes. Why was I doing this? This was insane. I knew my parents didn't want me to ride on a motorcycle. And I didn't even know where Mike was taking me. He said we were going to his house, but where was that? Where did he live? I knew nothing about him.

The bike was moving. I opened my eyes. This was kind of exciting.

Before I knew it we were pulling into a driveway. Mike's presumably. There was a minivan in the driveway. I hadn't considered that his mom might be home. It just seemed like Mike was the kind of person who went home to an empty house after school. But then again, I was the kind of person who went to an empty house after school. And Mike was nothing like me.

Mike parked the bike and I got off and handed him his helmet.

"See, I told you it'd be fine," he said.

"It was actually kind of fun." I blushed at the thought of how closely I'd been pressed against him.

"Maybe you'll ride with me again sometime."

"Maybe," I said. Or maybe once was enough.

"Come on inside. I don't know if we have any hot chocolate, but I'm sure we can find something you like."

So, I followed Mike into the suburban center-hall colonial that did not look like the kind of house that Biker Mike would live in. What had I been expecting, a tenement somewhere? Did we even have tenements in our town? And how run-down would an apartment have to be to qualify as a tenement anyway?

Inside was the kind of chaos that can only reign when small children live in a home. There were two boys playing video games, a small girl riding a tricycle in the hallway and another young girl standing on the stairs and yelling at the top of her voice for no particular reason.

"Madeline, be quiet," Mike said calmly.

The girl on the steps stopped yelling.

"Don't run into Emma, Julie," he said to the girl on the tricycle.

Julie got off her tricycle and came running over to Mike. "Give me a horsy ride, Mikey. Please."

"Later, pumpkin," he said.

"Are these all your brothers and sisters?" I asked.

"Let me check," he said.

I thought he was joking, but he snuck a peek at the two boys playing video games.

"Nope. Danny has a friend over, and I don't see Brian around."

His mom came into view, drying her hands on a dish towel. "Oh, good you're home, Mike. I was afraid I was going to have to bundle everyone up and take them all out with me. I have to go pick up Brian from a friend's house and drop Danny's friend back home. You'll stay here with the girls, won't you?"

"No problem," Mike answered as he took off his jacket.

I took off mine too; it looked like I'd be here at least until his mom came back.

From the other room one of the boys yelled, "I'm going with you."

"Yes, Danny, I know," she called back. "But we do have to go now. Boys, get your shoes on and your coats." She started to head back to the kitchen and then stopped and turned to me as if noticing me for the first time. She smiled and held out her hand for me to shake. "Hi."

I shook her hand. "I'm Emma."

Her smile got bigger as if she recognized my name. "Oh, so you're Emma. Nice to finally meet you."

Mike had been talking about me to his mother? Somehow I had imagined him as the uncommunicative type—especially with parents.

"I hope you two didn't have any big plans right now. I really do need you to watch Madeline and Julie."

"Just go already," Mike said, rolling his eyes.

Within minutes Mike and I were left alone with the two little girls. I didn't mind at all, it certainly made being here with Mike less awkward. Madeline and Julie, around three and four years old, reminded me of some of the kids I babysat for. How hard could this be?

"So, exactly how many kids are there in your family?" I asked as I leaned against the wall in the kitchen, next to a toy sink and stove.

"There're five of us." He was rummaging through a cupboard in the kitchen. I wasn't sure what he was looking for.

"I somehow pictured you as an only child." From a broken home, crying out for attention with the tattoos and the leather jacket.

"I was until about six years ago. Danny and Brian are my step brothers. Madeline and Julie are my half sisters." He looked up from his cupboard rummaging. "I don't see any hot chocolate mix, but I promised you a snack." He opened the fridge. "Is a Coke okay?"

"Sure, that's fine." I tried to chart his family tree in my head as he handed me a Coke.

I sat down at the table and tapped the top of the soda can, like Jake had taught me, before popping the lid open. So here we were, sitting in his kitchen. I had no idea what to say to him and apparently he had no idea what to say to me either, because we both just sat there looking at each other.

"I guess we could go over our lines," Mike said finally.

"I guess." I studied him. He was so unlike what I pictured the Captain looking like. "What are you going to do about your hair?" I asked suddenly.

He reached up and touched his shoulder-length hair. "Why? Is something wrong with it?"

"No. You just don't look very sea-captainish."

Mike shrugged. "I'll probably get it cut. That's still two months away, and Mom's been bugging me to get a hair cut anyway. No big deal."

Before I could say anything else the older of the little girls came running into the kitchen. "Julie's lost," she said, breathlessly.

Mike frowned. "What do you mean 'lost'?"

"I can't find her."

I suppose that would be the definition of lost.

Mike didn't look too concerned; apparently this kind of thing happened around here. "Where did you last see her?"

"We were playing hide and seek."

"And she's hiding?"

"No. I was hiding. When she didn't find me, I went looking for her."

Only a few minutes ago the kid had been riding her tricycle in the hallway, how lost could she be?

"Maybe she thought she was supposed to be hiding, Madeline," Mike said.

"Maybe. She is easily confused," she said, one finger on her chin.

I almost spit out my soda. But I recovered myself and started thinking like a babysitter. "You don't think she went outside do you?" I asked Mike. It was too cold for a little kid to be stuck out there for long.

Mike frowned. "I don't think she can open the door."

"Sure she can," Madeline said.

Mike stood up quickly. "I'll check outside first, just in case. Emma, you can look around in here."

"Does she have any favorite hiding places?" I

asked, following Mike into the front hall, where his coat was hanging. "And does she giggle when she hides?" Some of the kids I babysat did that.

"Nope, perfect silence," Mike said and slipped his coat on.

Great. That would make this *so* easy. Hah.

As he opened the door, I heard a sound. "That sounds like water running."

Mike stopped and listened for a second, then he shut the door and ran up the steps two at a time. "Sounds like it's coming from the master bath."

With Madeline trailing behind me, I followed Mike upstairs, through his parents' bedroom to the bathroom. And there was Julie, fully clothed, standing in a giant whirlpool tub, with the water running, a look of glee on her face.

Mike scooped her out of the tub while I turned off the water. At least she hadn't plugged the drain; the water wasn't filling the tub.

"You little monkey," he said. "Are you trying to take a bath with your clothes on?"

She giggled. "I hiding."

"You were supposed to be seeking," Madeline said with an air of disgust.

"Let's get you into dry clothes," Mike said.

I helped him get Julie out of her wet things and dried off. "You monkey," Mike repeated. "You know you're not supposed to go in the tub without Mom or Dad there."

"I hiding," she repeated with a giggle.

Mike just shrugged. We shepherded the girls downstairs where we could keep an eye on them and went back to our snacks. We sat back down at the table and Mike sighed, letting his shoulders slump.

"You were really worried about her, weren't you?" I asked. This was a new, softer side of Mike. One I hadn't expected to find, one that intrigued me.

"Well, sure," he said, a bit gruffly. "She's little. I don't want anything to happen to her on my watch."

Or at all. I smiled to myself. Mike was a softy. Who knew?

"So, should we go over lines?" Mike asked after a minute. But he didn't sound enthusiastic.

"Nah," I answered. "I kind of don't want to think about the play for a little while." I looked at him thoughtfully as I drank my Coke. He opened a bag of chips and held it out to me. I took one. I looked at it, instead of at him when I spoke. "You're not at all what I thought you were like."

"Oh, you mean, you just thought of me as 'big bad Biker Mike'?"

I froze, the chip halfway to my mouth. Oh, man. He knew we called him that? "I don't know about the big bad part," I muttered, not looking at him.

"Ah, but you don't really know me. Maybe 'big and bad' are the perfect ways to describe me."

Now I did look at him. He didn't look angry, just insolent with one arm wrapped around the back of the chair. "I don't think so," I said and ate the chip.

"Why not?" He was looking at me too intently.

"You care about your little sisters," I answered. He wasn't big and bad. I knew he wasn't. We'd been wrong about him at school.

He held out the chips bag again and I took another. "I guess that makes as much sense as deciding I'm no good because I ride a bike." He took a swig of his soda. "But how do you know you're right?"

I took a sip of soda too, so I wouldn't have to answer that question. I didn't know, did I? I avoided the topic all together. "Were you in the school play at your old school?"

Mike raised his eyebrows at the sudden change in topic, but he answered. "Yeah. We did *Camelot*."

"I'd love to play Guinevere."

"Yeah, I could see you as Guinevere," he said, his blue eyes boring into me.Why when he said that did I imagine not only myself as Guinevere but

Trevor as Arthur and Mike as Lancelot? That would make Trevor the husband I was trapped with, and Mike the man I truly loved. I felt my face turning red and shook my head to rid it of the thought. "What part did you play?" I asked.

"I was Lancelot."

I nearly choked on my soda. If my face wasn't red before, it was now. "That's a great part," I managed to splutter. "I like the song 'C'est Moi,'" I added lamely. I needed to banish the thought of me as Guinevere with him as Lancelot from my mind.

"Me too," he said, "though I wanted the part of Mordred. 'Seven Deadly Virtues,' is one of my favorite songs."

I didn't look at him; I concentrated on my soda.

"Purity, honesty, chastity, fidelity. They're all overrated."

What? I looked up quickly. What did he mean by that? Was he talking about me and Trevor?

"The deadly virtues. Get it?" he said with a half smile on his face. "From the song." He shrugged and took a drink of his soda. "I thought I was better suited to the part of Mordred anyway."

"Why? I bet you were a great Lancelot."

"Do you know the show?" he asked. "Don't you think I have more the look for Mordred? Big bad Biker Mike, playing the bad guy?" Mike gave me a crooked smile.

I blushed. "I guess, judging just by that, you'd be a good Mordred."

"Good thing that wasn't the only thing they judged on."

Good thing. And that's what I'd been judging him on, hadn't I? I didn't like myself very much right then. This conversation was getting too awkward and personal. Maybe we should have rehearsed our lines after all.

"So, how long have you been dating McGrath?" Mike asked.

Talk about awkward and personal, why was he talking about Trevor all of a sudden? “He’s been my boyfriend for almost a year now,” I said.

Trevor and I had been leaving the auditorium after a rehearsal one day and he’d turned to me and said, ‘Since Harry is supposed to be in love with Jean, maybe we should go out sometime.’ I had looked at him blankly for a moment and then, realizing he was asking me out, I accepted. And thus a romance was born.

“I wouldn’t figure him for your type,” Mike said. “I know he follows you around like a puppy dog, but what I can’t figure out is why you want him to.”

Why wouldn’t I want him to? Trevor walked me to classes, sat with me at lunch, called every evening on my cell phone so he could say goodnight, and e-mailed me things he thought I’d find funny. He’d written me poems and he smelled like mint when he kissed me. He sang “Sixteen Going on Seventeen” to me in the hallway. But I couldn’t say any of those things to Mike.

“What do you think my type is?” I asked, but didn’t give him a chance to answer. “Besides, Trevor and I have stuff in common, like the play.” I thought of his floppy blond hair, his soft brown eyes, and the dimple when he smiled. “And he’s really cute,” I added, and immediately wished I hadn’t.

“You are very superficial. Aren’t you?” Mike asked calmly.

I nearly spit out my soda. I should just stop drinking, it was dangerous around here. “What?” I put the can down and stood up, both hands on the table in front of me. “How can you say that?” I sputtered. “What right do you have to judge me like that? You don’t really know anything about me.”

“It’s true, isn’t it?” Mike asked, not looking in the least alarmed at my outburst. “You thought I was a big bad biker dude because of the way I look. You think Trevor is perfect because of the way he looks. Wouldn't you call that superficial?"

"No."

Yes.

Darn. I sat back down, deflated. Trevor was undeniably cute, but that wasn't all I liked about him. "He's also very nice and sensitive. He writes me poems," I said, not looking up from the table.

"Very sweet." Mike didn't sound impressed. "He strikes me as kind of a jerk."

It was true that Trevor wasn't very nice to Mike. "He's not," I assured. "What difference does it make to you anyway?"

Mike shrugged. "I don't know. I was just curious."

Why should he be curious about me? What possible difference could it make to him who I date? I didn't care who Mike dated. Did he date? I don't remember seeing him hanging out with any girls at school.

"I don't see that it's any of your business," I said, staring at the table. There was a blue stain on it that looked like someone colored it with permanent marker.

"I guess it's not really," Mike said matter-of-factly. "I wonder how he and Sara are getting along."

Oh, geez. Trevor was hanging out at my house with my sister and I was here. Was I an idiot? I needed to go home, but unless I wanted to walk home in the sub-freezing temperatures, I had to stay here until Mike's mom got home. We couldn't leave the little girls unattended.

"I really should be getting back," I said.

Mike nodded as if he understood. "Naturally. My mom will be back in a few minutes, then we can go."

We sat in silence for a moment, simply waiting for his mom to come home so I could get out of there. Madeline came in and stood next to me. "Hey, Mike's friend. Want to hear me sing a song?"

I smiled. It would certainly be better than

sitting here in awkward silence with Mike. "Sure, what are you going to sing?"

She didn't answer. She just started singing the alphabet song. Soon Julie was standing next to her singing along. And when they finished, they went right into "Itsy Bitsy Spider."

As they were finishing, I heard the front door open. I looked expectantly at Mike.

"Yup," he acknowledged, standing up. "That's Mom. I'll take you home now."

"Bye, Mike's friend. Are you going to come again sometime?" Madeline asked.

Not if I can help it.

"We'll see," I hedged.

"And, Madeline," Mike said gently, "her name is Emma."

"Nice name," Madeline said approvingly.

I needed to get home and see what Trevor and Sara were up to. If someone was going to be alone in the house with Trevor, it should be me. At least as we rode home, I didn't have to worry about making small talk; it was all I could do to get Mike to understand the directions to my house as I yelled at him over the rushing wind.

We pulled up to the house at the same time Jake pulled into the driveway. I climbed off the back of the bike as Lauren got out of the station wagon.

I handed Mike his spare helmet. "Thanks for the ride," I said.

"Yeah," he said. "See ya tomorrow." He started his bike, backed up, and drove off.

Lauren grabbed me by the arm. "Are you crazy? What do you think you're doing riding a motorcycle, with him of all people?"

Jake just stood to the side, arms crossed, shaking his head.

I shrugged. It wasn't any of their business.

Chapter 6
"What a Duet for a Girl and Goatherd"

"What were you doing with Biker Mike?" Lauren asked again.

"Getting a ride home," I answered and headed toward the door.

"But you left a long time ago. Where were you?"

"What are you doing here anyway? I didn't think you were talking to me anymore?"

"I'm talking to you," Lauren said, as if insulted that I should suggest otherwise. It appeared neither of us were really answering the other's questions.

"It's cold. Let's go inside," I said, stamping my feet.

"You turning Biker Chick on us now?" Jake asked as he followed me to the front door.

"As if! We just went to his house for a bit." I reached for the doorknob. "I didn't want Trevor to think I couldn't trust him."

"Can he trust you?" Lauren asked.

"Yes!"

"You can't trust any guy. We're all jerks," Jake said.

Lauren rolled her eyes and punched him in the arm.

I opened the door. I could hear "Sixteen Going on Seventeen" playing in the family room. I looked toward the French doors, and then back toward Lauren who had come in right behind me. I grabbed her by the arm. "Don't tell Trevor I was with Mike."

She shook her arm free. "You want to lie to your boyfriend, that's your business not mine."

"It's not lying to not tell every detail."

"Whatever."

The French doors opened and Trevor came into the hallway. He took hold of my hand and gave me a quick kiss. "I'm glad you guys are back. Sara and I are done rehearsing, and I need a ride home." He looked at Jake. "You don't mind, do you, man?"

Jake jangled his keys. "I don't mind. I needed to take Lauren home anyway. We just stopped off to make sure everyone got home okay."

"You're leaving?" I asked. "I just got here."

Sara came out of the family room now. "I'm surprised you didn't follow us home. You actually trusted your boyfriend with me for half an hour." She crossed her arms and gave me a half smile. What was she up to?

"Of course I trust you," I answered. I was so glad Mike had convinced me not to rush home after them.

"Sara and I spent some time going over our scene." Trevor smiled in Sara's direction. "I think it's safe to say that she's feeling more comfortable with the role now."

Sara just kind of shrugged. "Trevor makes it easy. Mrs. Valente makes me nervous."

"And I promised her we would practice as often as she wanted," Trevor said. He looked so pleased with himself.

This was the Trevor I remembered from last year's play: enthusiastic and animated, dropping everything to do something relating to the play. This shared enthusiasm was what we'd built our entire relationship on. I'd been looking forward to this aspect of being in the play together, but now he was sharing this with Sara.

"That's great," I managed to say, hoping I actually sounded happy.

This year Trevor wouldn't be singing to me on stage. But Mike would.

Mike.

The heat rose in my cheeks when I thought of

him and our afternoon together. What right did I have to be jealous of Trevor and Sara when I had just been at Mike's house and riding on his motorcycle?

Jake jangled his keys again, "You ready, man?"

"Yeah." Trevor turned back to me again. "I'm sorry I didn't spend the afternoon with you. But there's a dance on Friday, right? We'll go to that."

"Sounds good." I flashed him a smile. How could I even be a little bit worried about me and Trevor?

"And will you be there too, Sara?" Trevor asked as he slipped into his coat.

"Oh, Sara doesn't go to school dances. She doesn't like them," I said.

"Maybe I will," Sara answered, as if simply to prove me wrong.

"You don't like school dances," I reminded her.

"I didn't think I'd like acting either, but you keep telling me to give things a chance. Maybe I'll give the dance a chance."

"Good for you, Sara," Trevor said, patting her arm and giving her a warm smile.

My stomach clenched and I shivered as I looked back and forth between Trevor and Sara. Romances could start in plays. Could they end too?

Jake walked out the door and Trevor followed.

"Later," Lauren said to me as she headed out after them.

Sara had already cleared out of the family room. I took my *The Sound of Music* CD out of the player, brought it back to my room, and started playing it—every song except "Sixteen Going on Seventeen." I didn't want to hear that right now.

I changed out of my uniform skirt into sweat pants and opened my computer to do some homework. The IM box pinged. It was Lauren. I smiled. She was done being mad at me. Things were back to normal.

LaurenOne: What's this with Biker Mike?
Broadway Baby: Nothing. Just a ride home. Like u & Jake
LaurenOne: You went to his house first
Broadway Baby: So did u.
LaurenOne: Mike is not one of us. Even if he is cute.
Broadway Baby: He's ok.
LaurenOne: He'll bring you down.
Broadway Baby: just a ride home.
LaurenOne: Don't let it happen again.
Broadway Baby: Y wld it?
LaurenOne: Just so we're clear
Broadway Baby: Gotcha.
LaurenOne: Good. Gotta go. Homework. We'll talk about this later. TTYL
Broadway Baby: TTYL

I sighed. I didn't need Lauren ragging on me about Mike. After all, there was nothing happening between us. We just were in the play together and he gave me a ride home. Big deal. How was that going to "bring me down?" What did she mean by that anyway?

Caitlyn called about fifteen minutes later. "So? Spill, girl. What's this I hear about you tooling around town on a motorcycle with Biker Mike?"

"He gave me a ride home," I answered. What was the big deal, anyway? It's not like he'd kissed me or anything.

"Okay, I admit he's like totally hot. But isn't he like a criminal or something?" Caitlyn asked.

"I don't think so." He really didn't seem like the big bad Mike we had imagined. "He seems pretty nice. We just don't know him yet."

"So you're planning on getting to know him?" Caitlyn asked.

"Don't you think that will be necessary, being in the play together and all."

When Caitlyn answered she sounded uncertain. “I suppose.” After a pause her tone brightened. “So how was riding on his motorcycle?”

I smiled at the memory. “Wild.”

“You going to ride with him again?”

“I doubt it,” I said.

“Yeah. He’s totally not your type.”

“No, of course not. Trevor is my type.”

“Totally!” Caitlyn agreed, then added almost ominously, “So you better back off from Biker Mike.”

I hung up feeling uneasy. Was it really such a bad idea to get to know Mike better?

The next day Trevor and I sat together backstage, fingers entwined, on the prop sofa while we waited for our cues.

“This is more like it,” Trevor said. “I like spending time backstage with you. I wish you didn’t have to spend so much time with Biker Mike in this play.”

“He’s okay,” I answered. Why did Trevor have to bring him up now and ruin the mood?

Mike was on stage with Lauren. She had returned to our lunch table today, but things still felt unsettled. It was like we needed to do something to clear the air and move forward again. I wish I knew what I could do, other than giving up the part of Maria.

I watched as Jake joined them on stage. Jake and Lauren had amazing chemistry together on stage. They seemed to be spending time together off stage too. Was this play letting Lauren fulfill her romantic dreams after all?

They sang their song: “How Can Love Survive” about how difficult it was for two millionaires to stay in love—because they didn’t have to struggle through poverty together. I snuggled closer to Trevor, but he stood up. “The end of this song is my cue. I need to be ready.”

So much for romance.

And soon I had to make my own entrance, leapfrogging across the stage with the children—and believe me, that took awhile to get right. But finally we did, and I stood in front of Mike and said, *"Oh, Captain. You're home!"*

He wasn't supposed to smile at me; it wasn't in the script. But those blue eyes of his were dancing, and I would have started to blush if the children hadn't rushed in with their lines.

We had a whole page of dialogue then, and I could almost feel electricity crackling between us as we read. Mrs. Valente only had to stop us once the whole time.

At the end of the scene Lauren and I had one of our few times on stage together. I wanted so much to just reach out to her and say, "You're my best friend, you always will be, let's act like it." But I was stuck with saying the lines in the script. And honestly that wasn't going well for me.

After Mrs. Valente stopped me for the third time and had me read my line again, Lauren lost it. "If you can't even read one stupid line right how are you going to do this whole part?" She didn't even try to keep the exasperation out of her voice.

That wasn't fair. I had a lot of lines, and I'd been doing pretty well with them, but Lauren was making me nervous. I knew she thought she could do it better than I could. "I suppose if you were Maria you wouldn't have any of these problems."

I was vaguely aware that we had everyone's attention now, but I didn't care.

Lauren put her hands on her hips. "That's right," she said, as if daring me to contradict her.

I was going to take that dare. "I've got a news flash for you. I can do this part. I can do it as well as you can. Maybe better. That's why I got the part and you didn't." I crossed my arms in front of me.

She stepped closer. I stood my ground. We needed to have this out, and while on stage in front of everyone might not be the ideal venue, it was what we had.

Lauren's eyes flashed. "You didn't even want the part."

"I want it now," I shouted back.

"Then get the freakin' line right already," Lauren said and went back to her spot on the stage.

"Fine, I will." I turned and went to my spot. And we did the scene again, and we did it just right, and Lauren winked at me as she left the stage. It was like a weight lifted off my chest. Maybe, just maybe, everything would be okay.

As we were getting ready to leave the theater, Mike came up to me. "We get to learn that folk dance tomorrow. How are you at dancing?"

Jake answered before I had a chance to. "Emma didn't learn to walk when she was little. She learned to dance. It's all she ever does."

I stuck my tongue out at Jake. "I love to dance," I said to Mike.

"Well, good then." Mike smiled at me, and I wished I knew what he was thinking as he left the auditorium.

"Speaking of dancing," Sara said, directing her attention to Trevor, who was standing next to me. "We better go practice our dance. Are you ready to go?"

"I thought there wasn't a dance in the play." She got a dance too?

"We don't just stand in one spot and sing," Sara answered.

Of course. "Where are you going?" I asked.

"I'm going to take the late bus to his house so we can practice our dance."

"Why can't you practice at our house?" We had the music, we had the space, why go all the way over to his house?

"Fewer distractions," Sara said.

Did they think of me as a distraction? But

maybe that was a good thing. Trevor squeezed my hand, and when I looked at him he smiled, so I really couldn't be annoyed.

He gave me a quick kiss and said, "I'll call you later."

And then they were gone. "There goes your boyfriend. Again," Jake commented.

"Shut up, Jake," I answered without much conviction, as I watched Trevor and Sara walk down the hall together, toward the buses.

Lauren and I followed Jake out to the car, and Lauren grabbed my arm to slow me down. Once Jake was safely out of earshot, she said, "What's up with you and Trevor?"

"Nothing," I answered. Jake was already out the main doors and they shut behind him. "Why?"

"He's kind of spending a lot of time with Sara." Lauren leaned against the door and waited for my answer.

I shrugged. "They're just practicing."

"What about you and Mike?" Lauren asked, her perfectly-tweezed eyebrows arched.

I looked around to see if anyone had heard her, but we were practically alone. "What do you mean?"

"It's like sparks fly when you look at each other," she said.

"No. They don't," I lied.

"It makes for good theater."

"And you and Jake?" I raised my own eyebrows. "There's enough electricity there to power the school."

Lauren actually blushed. Unlike me, who blushes all the time, Lauren was not prone to blushing. "Good theater," she said. "We better go. We don't want Jake to leave without us." She pushed open the door and we went out into the icy air.

"The song you guys are doing sounds great," I said as we approached the car. This was finally like having a normal conversation with Lauren again.

She smiled. “Thanks. It’s a fun song.” She adjusted her book bag on her shoulder. “I kind of like the part of Elsa.”

“It’s a good part,” I agreed.

“And, you…you’re doing a good job as Maria.”

I smiled; that was high praise coming from Lauren.

“That part’s going to keep you really busy,” she added.

“Yes it is.” I sighed and Lauren laughed with me as we climbed into Jake’s car.

Friday at rehearsal Mike and I went to the gym to learn the steps to the *Laendler*, an Austrian folk dance. The gym teacher, who was doubling as the choreographer walked us through the steps, a CD player supplying the music.

“First you must bow and curtsy to each other,” Miss Davis said.

We did, and somehow even doing that made me blush.

“Now, hold hands.”

I hesitated. Holding hands seemed a very intimate thing to do. But Mike took hold of my hand. His hand was big and warm. And it felt like there were calluses. Was that from working on his bike?

“Now, walk this way, to here, in time to the music.”

We worked our way through the song, laughing when we stumbled over each other. By the third time through it, it was like I’d been doing this dance my whole life.

I didn’t expect an old folk dance could feel so romantic. But at the end, when Maria is supposed to pull away from the Captain, feeling overwhelmed with an unfamiliar emotion, I wasn’t acting. I was feeling that unfamiliar emotion myself. It made no sense. After all, this was Biker Mike.

It must have been the dance.

Chapter 7
"Quaint and Bizarre as a Team Are We"

I was in my closet trying to pick out something to wear to the dance and, at the same time, trying to answer Lauren's texts about what she should wear. I grabbed a royal blue dance skirt and typed into my phone.

"duznt realy m@r."

And it didn't. Lauren always looked great. My computer pinged, letting me know I had an IM, so I checked to see what Caitlyn wanted.

JerzyGrl: RU wearing leggings & mini?
Broadway Baby: Dancing skirt. I like to twirl
JerzyGrl: U should wear leggings & mini
Broadway Baby: Y
JerzyGrl: cuz L & I r.
Broadway Baby: I'm doing my own thing
JerzyGrl: Is that Y you were hanging w/M?
Broadway Baby: Gotta go.

I logged off. I needed to get ready for the dance. My phone chirped. It was Lauren again—of course.

"u shd wear leggings n a mini."

Whatever. I liked my blue skirt that spun out in a full circle when I twirled. I had a top that went perfectly with it too. I put them on and spun in front of the mirror. Very satisfying.

Jake yelled upstairs that he was ready to leave. I ran a brush through my hair one more time, freshened my lipstick, and went downstairs.

Dad was sitting in his armchair by the fireplace, where a warm fire was burning. "I assume you're going to the Snack Shack after the dance," he said, looking up from the book he was reading.

"We always do," Jake said.

Dad pulled a twenty out of his wallet and handed it to Jake. This was also part of our ritual—getting extra snack money from Dad.

"I want you back here no later than 11:30," Mom said from the sofa. Her feet were tucked under her and she had a news magazine in her hand. "Remember you have Sara with you."

"I'm not a baby, Mom," Sara protested.

Mom smiled. "I know that, dear. Now go and have a good time."

As we headed out to Jake's car, he said, "Not too good a time, you two. I'll be keeping my eye on you both."

"I'll probably be sitting in the bleachers with Shelly," Sara said, getting into the backseat of the car, "just so you know where to look."

"And I can take care of myself," I said as I slid into the front seat.

"Yeah," Jake looked sideways at me and started the car. "That's why I'm going to be keeping an eye on you."

The parking lot was filling up when we got there. "Where are Lauren and Caitlyn meeting you?" Jake asked, pulling into a space by the fence.

"In the gym. I'm meeting Trevor by the ticket table." And when we got inside, there was Trevor, just where he said he would be, looking very neat in his cargo pants and polo shirt.

"I bought your ticket," he said.

"Thanks. That was really sweet."

He took my hand and we went on into the gym; Jake and Sara could get their own tickets.

The gym was decorated in some sort of aquatic theme with blue streamers and paper fish hanging from the ceiling. The only lights were on in the back, near the drinks and snacks, so the dance floor was appropriately dim. A DJ had great dance music cranked up, but no one was dancing. Everyone stood milling around, yet no one was moving to the music.

I looked around for Lauren and Caitlyn. If they were here they'd probably be dancing, but I didn't see them. I did see a guy with long hair and a leather jacket on the other side of the room. Mike? So he attended school dances as well as being able to act and sing. He was full of surprises.

I jumped as someone tapped me on the shoulder. I turned to see Lauren and Caitlyn in nearly identical leggings and minis.

"We've got to request some good music," Caitlyn said. "Something to get people moving. How about the 'Cha Cha Slide'?"

"Too early for that," Trevor said.

"No, it's not. Caitlyn's got the right idea. Come on." I grabbed Lauren and Caitlyn by the hands and we ran up to the DJ, who was grooving out to his music by his big speakers.

"You girls have a request?" he asked, in his big rumbly voice.

"Cha Cha Slide," we all called out at once.

"Let's give it a couple of minutes until more people are here," he said. "But I promise you, I'll play it soon."

Sweet. A good line dance always got people out on the dance floor. Of course, it didn't take that much to get me moving. The music the DJ was playing now was pretty good. I started moving to the beat. Lauren and Caitlyn joined me. I waved Trevor over, but he just shook his head. He was standing with his friend, Fin, just watching. Whatever. I was going to dance. I wasn't going to force him to.

Sara was sitting on the bleachers, just like she said she would. If she didn't want to have fun at a dance, that was her own business. But I was really surprised when Jake and Justin started dancing with us.

"You don't need to keep this close an eye on me," I hollered to Jake.

"Making sure you stay out of trouble," he answered.

Great. Just what I needed, my brother hanging out with me and my friends.

"Hey, Jake!" Lauren called to him, "Do you have any good dance moves?"

He grinned. "I've got plenty of them, sweetheart." He moved a little closer to Lauren.

Caitlyn and I raised our eyebrows at each other and kept moving. But then, Justin seemed like he was dancing more with Caitlyn, leaving me the odd man out. Which really wasn't right, because of the three of us, I was the one with the boyfriend.

I went and grabbed Trevor by the hand. "Come on. Dance with me."

"Yeah, in a minute," Trevor said. He pulled his hand free from mine. "Fin's showing me something on his phone."

I smiled at Fin, who was standing there looking faintly disreputable in his camouflage pants and boots. "You should dance too, you know. This is a dance, not an electronics expo."

Fin shook his hips and did a little quick tap with his feet. "There, I danced. Happy now?"

I rolled my eyes and turned my attention back to Trevor. "Part of our agreement is that you dance at the dances," I reminded him.

"I will. Just give me a minute. I'll be right there."

I went back over to Caitlyn and Lauren. It's not like they were really paired up with Jake and Justin.

"Where's Trevor?" Lauren shouted to me.

"Playing with Fin's new cell phone or something. He promised he'd dance soon."

And that's when, with a wink in our direction, the DJ announced that he wanted everyone on the dance floor for the Cha Cha Slide. "Let's get everyone out here—and get this party started!" he yelled.

The dance floor started to fill up. Lauren, Caitlyn, and I were front and center as people formed up into lines. I kept expecting Trevor to step up next to me, but the music started, and he wasn't there. Instead, when I turned around during the song, I was surprised to find I was standing next to Mike. I gave him a smile, and he winked at me as the song instructed us to stomp two times.

Before the song was over, Trevor was on my other side, making room for himself between me and Lauren. "Told you I'd dance," he called to me over the beat of the song.

That song ended, but most people stayed on the dance floor. Once again we were dancing in a group, only this time, Trevor was there too. And Mike. I moved a bit to make sure that Mike would feel included. Lauren turned her back to us and Caitlyn followed suit, purposely excluding Mike—and me—from the circle. Before I could do anything else, Trevor took me by the hands and started dancing with me exclusively. Mike drifted away.

My eyes followed him as he headed back toward the refreshments.

Trevor squeezed my hand. "What are you looking at him for? I didn't think you went for the bad boy type."

"I don't," I assured, giving my attention back to Trevor. He was my boyfriend after all.

"I heard he got kicked out of his last school for being in a gang."

I looked back over in the direction Mike had gone. Could that be true?

Lauren and Caitlyn turned back toward us, enfolding me once again in the midst of my friends. I forgot about Mike. We danced a few more fast songs, one merging seamlessly into another, and then the

DJ switched it up some, playing a song that was slow and romantic.

Trevor took me in his arms "This is more my style," he said with a grin. He put his mouth close to my ear. "Have I told you how great you look tonight?"

I smiled and leaned into him a little more. I liked dancing in a group, but there was nothing quite like being held close to someone and swaying to the music.

When the song ended, Trevor stopped dancing. "I need a break. Want to get a drink or something?" he asked.

I was thirsty; a break wouldn't be a bad idea. We headed to the snack table. Trevor grabbed a cup of soda and I grabbed an 8-oz bottle of water. I gulped the drink and looked around the gym. Sara was still sitting on the bleachers with a couple of her friends. How was she going to have any fun at a dance if she just sat all night?

I threw out the empty water bottle and turned to Trevor. "Ready to dance some more."

He smiled but shook his head. "I love dancing with you, Em, you know I do. But I can't keep up with you. I need a breather. Go ahead and dance." He looked over toward the corner. "I'm going to go chat with Nick and Fin for awhile."

"When you're ready, come find me," I said.

He kissed me on the tip of my nose. "I'll do that," he said.

I headed back to the dance floor and my friends. When the song ended, Lauren grabbed my hand and pulled me toward the bathrooms.

"Time to freshen up," she said.

Lauren went straight to the mirror and checked her make up. She pulled a lipstick out of her little purse and applied it. Caitlyn and I waited. I knew there was something she wanted to say. Lauren did not just pull me into the bathroom so we could watch her put on lipstick. Finally, she blotted her lips with a bit of paper towel and turned to us.

"Jake asked me to go to the Snack Shack with him after the dance," she said.

"You always go to the Snack Shack with us after a dance," Caitlyn said.

"Cait!" She rolled her eyes. "You are so not getting it!" She crossed her arms and leaned against the sink. "We were slow dancing and he said he hoped I was going to the Snack Shack afterwards because he didn't want this magical time with me to end."

I blinked at her a couple of times. "My brother said that?"

"Get over the fact that he's your brother. He's totally the hottest senior in this school."

"It's a pretty small school."

"Can't you even be happy for me?"

"I am happy for you." I put my hand on her arm. "I think it's great. It's what you were hoping for. It's just weird."

"At least I don't have to worry about you stealing him from me," she said with a grin.

"When have I ever stolen a boyfriend from you?" I asked.

All she said was, "Matt."

Oh yeah, sixth grade. Luckily we'd all moved on.

"Both of you with boyfriends," Caitlyn sighed. "Is there no hope for me?"

"What about Justin?" Lauren asked.

"Nah. He's nice and all, but not my type."

"Who is your type? Biker Mike?" Lauren laughed.

"I think he's too much of a bad boy even for me!" Caitlyn said as she reapplied her bright red lipstick. "Did you hear that he got kicked out of seven schools for doing drugs?"

"Seven?" I asked.

"Seven." Caitlyn held up two fingers to signify

scouts honor, even though she hadn't been in scouts since she dropped out of Brownies in second grade.

"I don't see why they even let him try out for the play," Lauren said.

"Because he can act," I reminded them. Gang activity? Drugs? Those things just didn't fit with the Mike I'd seen with his little sisters.

Lauren headed out of the bathroom and we followed, but instead of following her all the way to the dance floor, I went looking for Trevor. He was still with Fin and Nick; now they were playing some sort of game on Fin's new phone.

"Hey sailor," I said. "What about a dance?"

Trevor smiled at me. "Later. Okay?"

I gave him a mock salute and stopped by the refreshment table for some more water. Mike was there, taking a handful of chips.

"Hey," he said to me.

"Hey." Had he really been kicked out of all those schools?

"You're a pretty good dancer," he said.

"Oh. Thanks." I should return the compliment, but I didn't, I just took a sip of my water.

"The DJ is good," Mike said. "The DJs they used to get at my old school were lame."

"Where did you used to go to school?"

"St. Stan's in Staten Island."

"St. Stan?"

"Stanislaus. We like to be informal."

"Aah. And before that?"

"Our Lady of Mercy—until eighth grade."

"And that's it?" I knew those rumors had to be false.

"This is one school too many," Mike said. "If my stepdad hadn't gotten a transfer, I never would have left St. Stan's."

"But you like it here, right?" I took another sip of my water.

Mike shrugged. "Things are starting to look up."

I finished my water and threw out the bottle. The music was calling to me, urging me to move, to feel the beat. I gave a little wave to Mike and started back toward my friends. But this time they actually had paired up. Caitlyn, despite saying that Justin wasn't her type, seemed to only have eyes for him, and Lauren and Jake were slow dancing even though it was a fast dance.

Whatever. I just let myself get lost in the music. I danced with one group, then another—whoever seemed to be having the most fun. And then, without even realizing I was doing it, I was dancing with Mike. He winked at me and I smiled back. After another fast song, the DJ switched tack again and slowed the music way down to soft and gentle. I took a quick look to see where Trevor was. He was still in the corner talking to Nick and Fin.

People were pairing up. I moved toward the bleachers. I'd just sit this one out. But then Mike was in front of me, his arms open, and he grinned.

"Shall we?" he asked.

Why not? I smiled back at him, and stepped into his arms.

"Things are definitely looking up," Mike said, his mouth close to my ear.

Slow dancing with Mike was amazing. It was like doing the *Laendler*, that folk dance we learned today, only ten times better. He had very strong arms. I had realized that this afternoon at rehearsal, but I was surprised at how good it felt to be held by them now.

He smelled good. It was the same aftershave I'd noticed on him before.

When we danced our bodies moved together like we were made for each other.

"Emma," Mike murmured in my ear.

I looked up at him to answer.

And then Mike kissed me.

Chapter 8
"My Heart Wants to Sigh"

And I kissed him back.

I was in his arms. His lips were on mine. The world around us disappeared. There was no one here but me. And Mike. I held him tight. Mike's mouth was warm and soft on mine. My legs were like rubber. I held him tighter to keep from falling down.

The DJ started playing Michael Jackson's "Thriller," and the spell was broken. I backed up from Mike. What had I done? I'd been kissing Mike! He smiled at me. I just stood there. What had I done?

I turned from him and fled. I left the dance floor and headed straight to the bathroom. I splashed water on my face.

What had that been? That kiss had reached down into my insides and pulled. Wow. I splashed more water on my face.

But it was Mike.

Biker Mike.

What was I thinking? I was dating Trevor. What if Trevor had seen us? What if anyone had seen us? Someone must have seen us. We were there in the middle of the dance floor. Sucking face. Oh, my gosh. Someone had to have seen us. It was a small school. I knew everyone. Trevor knew everyone. Someone would tell Trevor. What would I tell Trevor when he asked me about it? He was sure to ask me about it.

I turned my back to the mirror and leaned against the counter. What was I going to do? I couldn't stay in here all night. Okay. Deep breath. It was simple really. I needed to go out there and pretend that it had never happened. I had not kissed Mike. I couldn't have. So it simply must not have happened.

I went back into the gym. Trevor was still over with Nick and Fin. He couldn't have noticed anything. He was still playing that stupid game. I breathed a sigh of relief and headed right to him.

"Nick and Fin, my darling boys, you don't mind if I steal this young man away from you. I feel the need to dance with him." I took hold of Trevor's arm, in my best imitation of a southern belle.

Nick, with his three-sizes-too-big shirt, and Fin, with his no-laces combat boots, both grinned.

"We don't want to stand in the way of true love," Nick said.

Fin made kissy noises.

Trevor just said, "Later, dudes," and willingly went with me. "You missed me, huh?"

"Terribly." It could have been true, if I'd been thinking about him while I'd been dancing with Mike. But now I was thinking about him and that's what mattered. We danced together the rest of the night. Fast dances and slow dances; just me and Trevor.

I didn't see Mike anymore, because I refused to look for him.

Before I knew it the DJ was announcing that this would be the last song. It was a slow song and Trevor pulled me into his arms. "This is the part I like best about dances" he murmured in my ear.

"I like it too," I answered, looking up to talk to him. He wasn't as tall as Mike.

He leaned forward and kissed me. It was a nice kiss. A gentle kiss. A sweet kiss.

It wasn't like Mike's kiss.

I had to stop thinking about Mike's kiss.

The lights went up and the mood was broken. When we got over to the bleachers to retrieve our coats, there was discussion about who would go in which vehicle over to the Snack Shack.

"If we don't get a move on, there won't be a table large enough for us," I pointed out.

"Okay, fine. Let's just go. If someone gets left behind, it's not my fault!" Jake said.

We trooped out into the cold night air. Lauren apparently had earned front seat privileges, so Trevor, Sara, and I squeezed into the back seat. Caitlyn went with Justin, again. Too bad he wasn't her type.

We were barely through the door of the Snack Shack when Lauren announced, "Emma and I have to go to the bathroom."

"We do?" I asked. She'd already told me all about her and Jake. What could be of such pressing importance now?

"Yes we do."

"Do I have to go to the bathroom too?" Caitlyn asked.

"Yes."

"How about me?" asked Sara.

"No, you're fine," Lauren answered.

"Good thing you're here to keep track of our bladder functions, I don't know if I could handle it myself," Sara deadpanned.

Lauren gave a half-hearted chuckle and Caitlyn and I followed her into the bathroom. As the door closed, I turned to Lauren. "What's all this about? Jake ask you to marry him now or something?"

She faced me, arms crossed. "You kissed him."

"I did not kiss Jake! Believe me!" I assured.

"That's not who I meant. And you know it."

The blood rushed from my head and I leaned against one of the pink sinks for support. She knew. She knew that I'd kissed Mike. Deep breath. Someone once said that the best defense is a good offense. I hoped it was true. "Trevor? Of course I was kissing Trevor. He's my boyfriend. Come on." I headed toward the door. "I want to make sure they order nachos as well as cheesy fries."

"What's all this about?" Caitlyn asked. "You didn't call us in here to tell us that Emma was kissing her boyfriend."

"Because that's not who I saw her kissing," Lauren said.

I stopped, my hand on the door handle. Darn. I was going to have to lie. "Your eyes were playing tricks on you," I said with a laugh as I walked back over to the sink. I might need its support again. "I wasn't kissing him. We were just dancing. It was a slow song. Maybe from a certain angle it looked like we were kissing or something. But, believe me, we weren't."

"Who?" Caitlyn looked from one to the other of us, her eyes wide. "Who did you see her kissing?"

"Biker Mike." Lauren practically spit out the words.

"Wow!" Caitlyn stepped back and her eyes widened in admiration. "I didn't think you went for the bad boys. Trevor is such a goody goody."

"I wasn't," I said.

Lauren shook her head sadly and put her hand on my arm. "You're a horrible liar, Emma."

"I'm not lying." I shook her hand off and turned to face the mirror. Ugh. I looked completely washed out. I dug around in my purse and found some blush and started applying it.

"Jake thinks you're making a big mistake," Lauren said, leaning against the other sink.

"Jake?" I dropped the blush back into my purse and stared at her. "Were you discussing me with my brother?"

Lauren shrugged and looked at me through the mirror instead of face to face. "We're a couple now," she said as if that somehow explained it all.

"You're a couple now? After one slow dance and an invitation for french fries?"

"He thinks Trevor is a much better match for

you than Mike," Lauren said.

"Good," I said and started looking for my lipstick. "Because I'm dating Trevor and not Mike. I'm thrilled my brother approves."

"Besides," Lauren handed me her lipstick. It wasn't my color but it was a nice gesture. "It's not like I had to tell Jake. He would have known anyway."

I paused, the lipstick poised above my upper lip. "What do you mean?" I asked slowly.

"Everyone knows. It was the talk of the night."

Darn.

"I didn't know," Caitlyn protested.

I gave the lipstick back to Lauren.

Okay, I had to do some quick thinking here. Someone once said that if you repeat a lie often enough, people would believe it. It might have been Hitler who said that, which was unfortunate, because I think I needed to follow that advice. I'd simply stick by my story. "It was a trick of the light." I headed toward the door. "It just looked like we were kissing. Nothing happened. We were just dancing."

That was my story and I was sticking to it. I opened the door, but stopped and turned back to Lauren and Caitlyn. "Do you think Trevor has heard those rumors?"

"I don't know," Lauren said. "Probably."

Time for a little damage control. I took a deep breath and headed back to the dining area.

The Snack Shack was crowded with post-dance St. Stephen's students. Our group was crowded into a corner booth. I sat down next to Trevor at one end, Caitlyn sat next to me, and Lauren sat next to Jake on the other end.

"We already ordered," Trevor said.

"Did you get cheesy fries *and* nachos?" I asked.

"Yeah. And Cokes for all three of you. Hope that's all right?" Jake asked, but he wasn't looking at me, he seemed to only have eyes for Lauren. This was going to take some getting used to.

Lauren fluttered her eyelids. "That's fine," she said sweetly.

I turned to Sara who was sitting in the curve of the booth between Trevor and Justin. "So what did you think of the dance?" I asked. "Are you glad you went?"

She shrugged. "The music was pretty decent."

"But you didn't dance to it," I pointed out.

"No. People watching was much more interesting."

My hands suddenly felt ice cold.

Trevor chuckled. "And what did you see?"

What *had* she seen? I had to remember to breathe.

"A little of this, a little of that," she said enigmatically. "People in the same room who can't talk to each other but text each other on their phones. Romances being born, romances ending." She smiled at me. She'd seen something, I knew she had. "It's amazing what you can learn by just watching."

Just then the food came. It was a welcome distraction since no one pressed Sara for any more details on the things she had learned.

"So," Jake said, dipping his cheesy fry into the salsa, "act II of the play should be interesting."

"You're getting cheese in the salsa," Sara said, slapping at his hand. "What's so interesting about act II?"

"Because that's when Emma gets to fall in love with Biker Mike and kiss him."

I froze with my hand half way to the nachos. Beside me, Trevor tensed. Casual and nonchalant, that was how this had to be played. "You're right. Lots of kissing in this play, isn't there? Trevor and Sara get to kiss in act I. Too bad you and Lauren don't get to kiss on stage."

"I imagine we'll find a way to make up for that off stage," Jake answered, draping his arm playfully over Lauren's shoulder.

"I don't know how you're going to do it," Lauren said, shaking her head. "I wouldn't want to kiss Mike."

"Good thing," Jake said and pulled her closer.

"Dylan told me that Mike got kicked out of his old school because he knifed some kid," Justin said.

"His stepfather got transferred," I said quietly.

"I swear he does drugs," Trevor said. "He's in my history class and he just sits there, his eyes glazed over."

"And that motorcycle. It's a piece of junk," Justin said and laughed.

"It's historic," I said under my breath.

"I'm glad he's not in my grade," Sara said. "He scares me."

"Yeah." Jake turned to Lauren. "You should be glad you didn't get the role of Maria. You'd have to kiss Biker Mike."

"I'm supposed to be in love with him when the play starts, remember?" Lauren said with a roll of her eyes. She took a sip of her Coke and looked directly at me. "That's bad enough. I don't know how you'll be able to stand it, Emma."

My face was burning. Mike was not the bad guy they were saying he was. But if I defended him, they'd wonder why. They'd think those rumors about me kissing him were true. I couldn't have that.

"I'm glad he didn't come to the Snack Shack with us today," Sara said. "I can never relax when he comes with us after rehearsal."

"I know," Caitlyn agreed. "It's like I'm always expecting him to put roofies in my drink or something."

Why would he do that? Why would they even think he would do that? I blinked back the tears that were threatening to come to my eyes.

Trevor put his arm around me. “It’s too bad you have to kiss him in the play,” he said. “But you’re a good actress, I’m sure you’ll be able to manage.”

I remembered the feel of Mike’s lips on mine and I shivered.

“Even Emma’s not that good an actress,” Lauren said.

I glared at her and Trevor held me a little tighter. “You’re scaring her now. Don’t worry, Em. We’ll all be around to make sure nothing bad happens.”

“What could possibly happen?” I asked.

“You could start to like it,” Caitlyn said.

“That would never happen, right Emma?” Trevor asked. Was there a hint of a threat in his voice?

“Of course not,” I answered. But that kiss had reached deep inside of me. I would do almost anything to be kissed like that again.

“Because really, he’s skeevy,” Lauren said.

“I don’t think he should hang out with us after the rehearsals anymore.” Trevor reached for another fry.

“But he’s part of the play. It’s not fair to exclude him.”

“It’s hardly like the whole cast goes out after the rehearsals. He can find his own friends,” Trevor said.

And what could I do but agree?

Later that night when I was getting ready for bed, Sara came into my room. “I know you kissed Mike.”

I flopped back onto my pillow. Of course she did. “He kissed me,” I said.

“Looked kind of mutual,” she answered, sitting in my saucer chair.

I just sighed and stared at the ceiling. Yeah. Kind of. It was.

“Does this mean you’re going to break up with

Trevor?" she asked.

"No," I said quietly. "Trevor's a great guy, a great boyfriend. I'm not going to lose everything with him because of one kiss." Not even if it was a great kiss, which it was.

"So, what are you going to do about Mike?" Sara asked, and her voice was gentle, not accusing like Lauren had been.

A tear slipped out of my eye, but I ignored it. "I don't know. Nothing I guess. Just stay away from him."

Sara didn't say anything, so I sat up so I could see her.

She nodded thoughtfully. "Let me know how that works for you as you have to pretend you fall in love and get married."

"Acting. All acting," I said.

"Emma," Sara said, and now she sounded a little sad. "I know you. When you get into a role, you really get into it. You can't separate yourself from it that much. You played a role where you were supposed to be marrying Trevor, and you're still dating him a year later. You spent two weeks pretending to be Liesl before the auditions and calling Trevor, Rolf." She looked at me for a moment. "So what are you going to do?"

"I'll think about it tomorrow," I said. "Tomorrow is another day.'"

"Tres cliché." Sara rolled her eyes and got up to go. "Good luck," she said as she shut the door behind her.

I had a feeling I was going to need it.

Chapter 9
"And Taste My First Champagne"

I woke up Saturday morning and stretched luxuriously. An incredible dream was still threading itself in and out of my brain. I didn't want to let its hold on me go completely. A dream of walking on the beach, hand in hand with a cute guy.

I replayed the scene in my mind: the rhythmic and soothing sound of the surf, the cool feel of wet sand squishing beneath my toes, the smell of the salt water, that unique beach smell, me in an adorable floral bathing suit with a matching long pareo for a cover-up, my fingers entwined with those of a guy in a blue and white bathing suit, no shirt, an Eagle tattoo on his arm, his long hair flowing freely in the gentle breeze.

Tattoo? Long hair? I sat up quickly. I had dreamed about Mike. No. I couldn't be dreaming about Mike. It had to be Trevor in the dream. I tried to re-imagine the scene with Trevor there—short blond hair, no tattoo—but I was forcing it.

The dream had definitely been about Mike, but I couldn't think about him. I especially couldn't think of that kiss last night. That kiss had been awesome.

No.

That kiss was off limits. I could not think about it.

I couldn't *not* think about it.

I had a date with Trevor tonight. He was the guy I had to spend my time thinking about.

When Trevor's dad dropped us off at the mall movie theater, Trevor said, "I was thinking we could see *Three's A Crowd*."

"But that's a romantic comedy." He always wanted to see action or adventure.

"I know. I thought we'd go see something you'd like."

"That's so nice." I gave him a quick kiss on the cheek. "I'd like that."

Trevor bought the tickets while I bought us some popcorn and soda. When we went into the theater, we headed straight to the back, to the make-out seats.

"What's this movie about?" Trevor asked as he took some popcorn.

I tried to remember what I'd seen in the trailers and in the paper. "It's about a girl who's about to get married and instead falls in love with the bartender at her bachelorette party."

"Same old story," Trevor said.

"What? It's hardly an every day occurrence that someone falls in love with someone else on the eve of their wedding."

"But people are always falling in love with people they're not supposed to," Trevor pointed out. "Even in *The Sound of Music.* Maria is supposed to be a nun—in love with God—and she falls in love with the Captain."

I suppose there was some truth to that. "It's a good thing I fell in love with the right guy," I said, and put my hand on his arm.

He put his hand over mine. "I'm sorry I kind of ignored you for part of the dance yesterday."

"That's okay."

"No. It's not." Trevor sat back in his seat and stared at the ads running on the screen for a few minutes. "If I'd been with you then those stupid rumors couldn't have started."

My heart started to beat too fast. "What rumors?" I asked, keeping my voice steady with some effort.

"They're really stupid. Probably people jealous

because you got the lead in the play. But people were saying you were kissing Mike."

"Anderson?" I asked, stalling for time.

Trevor turned to me and raised one eyebrow. "How many Mikes do you know?"

"It's not that. It's just that the whole idea is so ludicrous." I swallowed. Did I sound natural when I said that? Would he believe me?

"It's just, I know you guys are going to spend a lot of time together in the play—and that's how we started out—and I don't want to lose you." His voice actually caught as he finished speaking.

I reached out for his hand. "You're not going to lose me." And this time I knew I wasn't lying. I may have kissed Mike, and I may have really enjoyed it, but I had no intention of dumping Trevor in favor of Mike.

The lights dimmed and the movie started. We watched and munched on popcorn for awhile before Trevor moved the popcorn container to the floor and put his arms around me. We didn't watch too much more of the movie after that, which was okay, because this particular movie hadn't been the best idea. The girl did fall in love with the bartender who was a clear case of "not her type," but she fell in love anyway. And the perfect guy turned out not to be perfect for her.

But that wouldn't happen to me.

Trevor walked me to the door when his father dropped me off, and said, "I knew those rumors about you and Mike couldn't be true. He's totally not your type."

I smiled at my boyfriend. "Exactly," I said. "You're my type."

"I'm glad." He gave me a long kiss, even though his dad was probably watching from the car.

When I went inside there was a light on in the family room, so I went that way. Mom and Dad were curled up together on the couch watching some old movie.

"I'm home," I said.

Mom looked up.

Dad paused the movie. "Did you have a good time?"

I shrugged. "Good enough. The movie was kind of lame. But funny."

"True of so many movies," Dad said with a sigh. "They just don't make them like they used to."

I rolled my eyes. Here we go, Dad's favorite topic.

"Where are the classics like *Gone with the Wind* and *Casablanca*? Do you know how many great quotes came out of *Casablanca*? And they used to be able to tell a good story without having to have nudity and vulgarity. Don't people have any creativity anymore?"

"I think you were born about fifty years too late, Henry," Mom said. "But then, if you were born fifty years earlier, you'd probably complain that these talkies are ruining the moving pictures."

"Ha, ha, you just don't appreciate greatness."

"I appreciate you, dear," Mom said. This was an old conversation, one that got rerun over and over.

I figured I'd heard enough. "Well, good night."

They didn't waste any time turning their movie back on. It wasn't *Casablanca*, but it was an oldie: *The Philadelphia Story*. The story of someone falling in love with someone else on the eve of her wedding—actually, realizing that she was still in love with her first husband. Was that the only story line out there?

I flopped down on my bed. If all these movies and stories were true, then it was possible that I could fall for Mike. Isn't that the lesson these movies were trying to portray? But there was nothing between me and Mike. Just one kiss. One little kiss.

One really awesome kiss.

In the play, Mike and I have to fall in love. I

mean, Maria falls in love with the Captain. I do know how to separate reality from fiction.

But that had been an incredible kiss last night.

I needed to stop thinking about Mike.

I picked up *Jane Eyre.* Maybe doing some homework would distract me. Before long I tossed the book down on my bed. Romance had never been easy, had it? Not for Romeo and Juliet, not for Jane Eyre and Mr. Rochester, not for Maria and Captain von Trapp, not for me. Maybe what I needed was sleep.

****

Monday morning, I started the daily struggle with my locker and developed my strategy if I should encounter Mike. I would play it cool. I would not get flustered. And most importantly, I would not blush.

"Want a hand with that?"

I looked up at Mike, saw that beautiful mouth, and remembered how it had felt on mine. I missed the next number completely as the dial spun out of control. I could feel my face turning about fifteen different shades of pink.

"Um, no, I think I've got it," I stammered. I started turning the dial again. "I, um, I don't need anything in there anyway."

"Planning on wearing your coat all day?" Mike sounded amused.

How dare he laugh at me? "Um, no." I refused to look at him again. "I guess I do need to get into it."

"Step aside and let me at it."

"No, really, I can do it." I don't know why I insisted. After all, it was clear by now that I would never get the best of this locker.

"About the dance…" Mike started quietly.

"No." I didn't want to hear what he might have to say about that. I just couldn't let myself think about that kiss. Or look at him.

"Jiggle the handle when you get to the last number," he offered as helpful advice.

I nodded. But even trying that didn't work. I just rested my head against my locker. I surrender.

A hand rested on my shoulder. "I wasn't really thinking," Mike said. I knew he was talking about the kiss. "But I'm not sorry."

I wasn't sorry either, not really. But I couldn't say that. The hand moved off my shoulder. I thought he walked away, but then I was aware of someone leaning on the locker, hovering over me.

"Just go away," I muttered.

"If that's what you want," Trevor said.

Trevor? I straightened and saw him, starting to move away. "No," I called out. "I didn't mean you. I thought you were Mike."

He stopped. "Mike?"

I could feel a headache coming on. "He was offering to help me with my locker."

"I wish he'd leave you alone," Trevor said. He put his arm around me protectively. I still needed to get into the locker so I shrugged him off. I spun my dial frantically as the warning bell rang. Trevor looked at his watch.

"You don't have to wait if you're worried that you might be late," I said.

"I don't mind." But he looked at his watch again.

Finally, after two more tries the locker opened. I crammed my coat in, grabbed the books I needed, and Trevor walked me to homeroom. It was not an auspicious start to the day.

****

That afternoon, Trevor was at my locker before I was. He waited patiently while I tried my lock four or five times before it opened and then stayed close by my side as we headed to the auditorium. At least all this attention from Trevor was making it easier to avoid Mike.

But I couldn't stop thinking about Jake's comment on act II. That I had to kiss Mike. We had finished blocking out act I on Friday. Today we would start act II. I flipped through my script as I sat next to Trevor in the front row of the auditorium. Where was the kiss? I found it in scene five. Maybe we wouldn't get that far today. Maybe I'd have a reprieve.

Then Mrs. Valente announced we were going to do act I again. With a sigh of relief I shut my script. There was nothing romantic between the Captain and Maria in act I. Well, except for the dance.

The nuns trooped up on stage and we got started. I went backstage to wait for my cue. Once I was on stage singing and simply being Maria, all my other concerns washed away. There was no illicit kiss to hide from my boyfriend, no locker that refused to open. I was Maria. This was why I loved being on stage.

By the time rehearsal ended, I was exhausted. I couldn't wait to get to the Snack Shack and have a cold drink. No hot chocolate for me today. I needed a Coke.

As Trevor was helping me on with my coat, Mike came up to us. "So, is everyone heading to the Snack Shack now?"

"Totally," I said.

But Trevor butted in. "Not today, man." Then he steered me toward the doors.

"We're not going?" I asked. "What are we doing instead?"

"We're going," Trevor said quietly. "We just don't want the hoodlum with us."

I wanted to say that if they would just give him a chance, get to know him, they would find that he wasn't a hoodlum. But if I said anything it would just make it seem like those rumors that I kissed Mike were true. I didn't want that.

Once we were settled into a booth at the Snack Shack Jake wrapped his arm around Lauren and pulled her close. They then proceeded to whisper and giggle (well, Lauren was doing the giggling, not

Jake) to each other as if the rest of us weren't there. Caitlyn was chattering on about the dress she'd seen in a magazine the other day that she just had to have, and Trevor, although he was holding my hand, was deep in conversation with Sara about some aspect of their scene together.

I looked around at the retro Coca Cola pictures on the wall and then I saw him. Standing by the take out counter; watching us. Biker Mike. He turned and caught my eye. I immediately looked down at the white and black flecked linoleum of the tabletop.

When I looked up again he was leaving. Could I just let him leave like that? Shouldn't we invite him to join us?

"Mike's here," I said.

"Can't that guy take a hint and leave us alone?" Trevor said.

"Yeah," said Lauren. "It's not like this is the only place you can hang out after school."

I couldn't think of any place else anyone hung out.

I guess asking Mike to join us was out of the question. I thought of my dream and watched through the window as he got on his motorcycle and rode away.

"I wish he would just get kicked out of the play," Sara said, taking a french fry and waving it around like a pointer. "Criminals shouldn't even be allowed to try out."

"I don't think he's ever been in trouble at St. Stephen's," I pointed out.

"He's just too slick to get caught," Trevor said. "I'm sure that if he were caught doing something illegal, he'd be out in a minute. Probably out of the school too. St. Stephen's has an image to uphold after all."

"Shouldn't it be an image of Christian charity? Shouldn't we welcome strangers?" I found myself asking. My head hurt. I wanted to go home and rest.

Lauren looked up from whatever private conversation she and Jake were having. "You keep sticking up for him and people aren't going to want to hang around with you either," she said, with an arch of her eyebrow.

"Yeah," Sara said. "They'll think you really were kissing Mike at the dance."

And I couldn't have that, could I?

Chapter 10
"Ford Every Stream"

Tuesday we didn't have rehearsal because Mrs. Valente was sick. Jake and Lauren decided to take this opportunity to go someplace alone, so, as Jake informed me, Sara and I would have to find our own way home. The cold spell had broken, so walking home wasn't a problem. Sara found me and told me she was going home with Shelly on the bus and she'd see me later. Trevor and Caitlyn had already caught their bus. I was on my own.

And I couldn't get my locker open. I spun the dial fruitlessly a few more times and then punched the metal. The locker didn't open, but I did hurt my hand. Maybe I should just ask for a new locker.

The halls were emptying out. Soon I'd be the only student left and they'd lock the building up and I'd be stuck here all night. I'd probably even starve to death. And all because of my stupid locker.

I heard the sound of a locker opening near mine, so I wasn't alone yet. I looked over and there was Biker Mike. He didn't look at me. He was probably upset about yesterday. I would be.

I walked over to him and leaned on the locker next to his. "Um…hi," I said.

He barely looked at me before putting more stuff in his locker. "Hi."

I stood there and looked at my shoes. What should I say? Tell him my friends didn't want to hang out with him? Say I was too chicken to stand up for him?

He shut his locker and looked at me. "Is there something you want?"

I scuffed my shoe against the floor and didn't look at him as I asked, "You want to go over lines today, since there's no rehearsal or anything?"

He didn't answer right away. I thought maybe he was just going to leave without saying anything. I couldn't really blame him if he did.

Finally he said, "It's kind of chaotic at my house—as you know. Where do you suggest we go?"

I let out a huge sigh of relief. He wanted to rehearse with me. He wasn't mad. I looked up at him and smiled. "My house is free. Want to go there?"

He nodded slowly. "Sure. We can do that."

Of course I still had to get into my locker before I went home. We walked to it together.

"Are you sure you're allowed to be seen with me?" Mike asked.

I looked around the empty hallway. "I don't see anyone objecting. Do you?" It only took me two more times to get the lock open and then we headed out to the parking lot. I was going to have to ride Mike's bike again, unless I wanted to have him slowly follow me home while I walked, which seemed ridiculous.

I didn't have nearly the trouble getting on the bike this time that I did the first time. I might actually get to like riding a motorcycle. Especially on a day like today when the weather was not in the sub-freezing range.

We got to my house and went inside.

"Want a snack?" I asked.

"Sure," Mike said, following me to the kitchen. "No one's home?"

Was it a mistake to come home alone with him? What if those rumors about him had been true? I opened the refrigerator and took out two cans of Coke. "Sara went home with Shelly, and Jake and Lauren went off to practice being a brand new couple."

Mike popped the top on his soda. "What about

your parents?"

"Working." I grabbed a bag of pretzels out of the pantry. "Let's go into the family room." I pointed through the glass doors off the kitchen.

"So, no one's home when you get home?" he asked.

"Last year Mom was still working part-time, when Sara was in eighth grade. But she figures now that we're all in high school, she can trust us alone for a few hours a day."

"Can she?" he asked and sat on the sofa.

"Sure."

"You mean you're not secretly some 'bad girl' under that Catholic school girl exterior?" I knew he was joking by the chuckle in his voice.

"Hardly," I laughed.

"Too bad," he said.

I laughed some more. "You're one to talk. You're the good Catholic school boy under the bad boy exterior."

He put his finger to his lips. "Shh. I don't want my cover blown."

I ran my finger around the rim of the soda can. "Why?" I asked finally, no longer laughing.

He stopped laughing too and shrugged. "Keeps people from bugging me, I guess."

"Wouldn't you rather have friends?"

"With the snobs at St. Stephen's? No thanks."

I sat up a little straighter. "It's not all snobs."

"No?"

I thought about yesterday, how Trevor had lied to him in order to keep Mike from hanging out with us, and I blushed. "Maybe we should go over our lines." I dug my script out of my backpack.

"Probably a good idea," Mike said.

We went over our parts from act I trying our best to include the stage direction that Mrs. Valente had given us for various scenes.

When we finished Mike said, "Want to move on

to act II?"

"Sure." I waved my script in the air. "Let's live dangerously." My cell phone chirped, indicating a text message. It was from Caitlyn. Just a generic, "What's up?" She was home from school and bored. But if I told her what I was really doing, she'd give me a hard time, and if I let her think I wasn't doing anything she'd wonder why I didn't feel like texting her right now.

"Anything important?" Mike asked.

"Just Caitlyn. Bored. Wants to chat."

"That girl can sit still long enough to type in a text message?" Mike asked, stretching his arm out along the back of the sofa.

"It's only two words." I looked at the phone. I needed to send her some sort of reply. "What do I tell her I'm doing?"

"Planning wild and nefarious deeds with a known criminal," he said with a smirk.

"Uh huh." I sat down next to him on the sofa.

"I'll answer her for you," he said and made a move to take the phone from me.

I held it out of his reach. "No. You won't!" Quickly I typed in that I was doing homework and I'd talk to her later. As soon as I sent it, the phone rang.

"My you're the popular one this afternoon," Mike said.

I looked at the incoming number. Trevor. My stomach started to feel funny. What should I do now?

"So, who's that now? Lover boy?" Mike asked.

"Um, yeah. I better answer this." I pushed 'talk' and moved toward the kitchen, "Hi," I said brightly and closed the glass doors behind me.

"Hey, what's up?"

"Nothing, just doing some homework."

"I was thinking of ways to get Mike out of the play," Trevor said.

I quickly glanced through the family room doors. Mike was still sitting on the sofa, looking through his script.

"Don't," I said.

"Don't what?"

"Don't make things hard on him. He's not so bad."

"Well, you'd want everyone to think that—since they already think you kissed him at the dance—and I'm sure you don't want people thinking you've gone bad girl."

Without being able to see his expression and body language, I wasn't quite sure how to take that.

Before I could really reply, he laughed. "Anyway, I was kind of wondering if Sara was around, I thought I'd get my mom to drive me over and we could practice our scenes."

"She went to Shelly's," I said.

"I don't have to tell that to my mom," Trevor said and I could almost hear him wink. "I could still get her to drive me over."

Another quick glance at Mike going over the script in the next room. "Not today." I tried to make sure I sounded really regretful. "I'm trying to get caught up on a lot of homework."

"Maybe tomorrow then, if Mrs. Valente is sick again."

"Maybe."

I got off the phone then and went back to the family room. My stomach was in a knot. But there was nothing wrong with rehearsing with Mike. After all, Trevor had wanted to rehearse with Sara. But I felt like I was hiding something, and since I hadn't told him Mike was here in our house, I guess I was.

Mike didn't ask about my phone call with Trevor, he just said, "So, should we start from our first scene in act II?"

"Sure." I picked up the script and found the right place. We hadn't blocked these scenes out yet, so we didn't have to worry about any stage direction. We just sat on the sofa and read our lines. There was one bit of stage direction that was a little more difficult to ignore.

"I'm supposed to kiss you here," Mike said.

I looked at my script. The words "they kiss" were like large blinking neon lights on the page. "I think we can skip that for right now," I answered.

"Might be for the best," Mike said.

When he didn't continue with the next line, I looked up at him.

He grinned at me. "Besides, I already know you can kiss."

My face flamed. "Yeah, um. You too," I said.

He laughed. "You're okay, Emma, you know that."

We finished going through act II and Mike stood up and stretched. "I better get going. I'll see you tomorrow at rehearsal."

"Yeah." I stood up too.

"But I guess not at the Snack Shack afterwards." His grin was a bit wry.

I was really embarrassed by my friends' behavior the other day. "You can come with us if you want." Though I wondered how that would really play out, and would it be a good idea to have Trevor and Mike in the same spot.

"Nah. I know when I'm not wanted."

"They just don't know you," I said.

"And don't want to." Mike slipped his leather jacket back on, threw his backpack over one shoulder, and put his helmet on. "Later," he said as he left.

That evening, when I really was doing my homework, my IM pinged. It was Lauren.

LaurenOne: What was Mike doing at your house this pm?
Broadway Baby: ?

When in doubt, play dumb.

LaurenOne: Saw his bike.
Broadway Baby: rehearsing
LaurenOne: Keep it at school.
Broadway Baby: Y? I rehearsed with T last year.
Broadway Baby:You rehearse with Jake.
LaurenOne: Totally different.
LaurenOne: And if you can't see that you have problems
Broadway Baby: Thks.
LaurenOne: Just trying to help you
Broadway Baby: Don't need help
LaurenOne: Em, I'm your friend. I just want what's best for you.
LaurenOne: Biker Mike is not best for you.
Broadway Baby: Whatev. Gotta go.
LaurenOne: You can't run away from this.

I could certainly try.

Broadway Baby: Jane Eyre beckons. TTYL
LaurenOne: TTYL

The next morning before homeroom, Lauren and Caitlyn cornered me at my locker.

"We need to talk to you," Lauren said.

Caitlyn stood there and nodded solemnly.

"What is this? An intervention?"

"Kind of," Lauren said. "We're concerned about you."

"Why?" I spun the dial on my lock. But, surprise, surprise, the locker didn't open. It wasn't even worth trying right now, I leaned against the locker, arms crossed in front of me, and waited for their answer.

"Trevor's getting suspicious. You've got to stop hanging out with Biker Mike."

"I wasn't hanging out with him. I was rehearsing."

"That's another thing," Caitlyn said, pointing her perfectly manicured finger at me. "You lied to me. Yesterday you said you were doing homework, but you were really with him. Something that has you lying to your best friends has to be bad news."

"We were just going over lines," I said softly. "Now, I need to get into my locker or I'm going to be late for homeroom." I turned from them and concentrated on my combination. Was Caitlyn right? I had lied to her. Maybe Mike was a bad influence on me.

That afternoon at rehearsal we really did start act II. The first scene was a very long scene—with two songs—and I was in most of it. I went backstage to await my cue.

We were still blocking out every movement on stage, which made the process very slow. Painfully slow. I read through my script while I waited and became so engrossed in it I almost missed my cue.

But someone called to me. I flipped back to the right spot in the script and started singing "My Favorite Things" off stage. Then I was on stage, and Mrs. Valente was stopping the children from rushing around me in order to have them stand in a different order. I sighed and made my entrance again. And again.

We continued singing the song all together, did a little dialogue, and then Mike was standing in front of me. I mean the Captain. And we were alone on the stage.

He said, "*You've come back.*"

And I couldn't remember my line. We had done this scene yesterday. But all I could think of was my friends' warning. If I was lying to be with Mike, then something was wrong, wasn't it? But that kiss. I'd been able to somehow not dwell on it yesterday, but today I just kept looking at that mouth and remembering how it felt to be kissed by him. But I couldn't think about that. I had to say something. I was the only other person on stage. I must have to say something. I remembered the script in my hand and looked at it.

"*Yes, Captain*," I answered, feeling all the blood rush to my cheeks.

Somehow I managed to stumble through the rest of the dialogue, and not surprisingly, we had to do the whole scene again, per Mrs. Valente. The second time through, I was able to concentrate on the part—and forget that this was Mike in front of me. This was the Captain standing here. I could do this.

Then finally, I was off stage. I sat in the audience next to Trevor. He held my hand as we watched Jake, Lauren, and Mike sing "No Way to Stop It."

"He scares you, doesn't he? That's why you were fumbling when you were up there," Trevor said quietly, his mouth close to my ear.

"No." But would it be better if he thought that was the case?

"You shouldn't have to put up with that." He rubbed his thumb against my thumb.

"It's not a problem. I just got a little flustered."

"It's because he scares you," Trevor repeated. "Did he threaten you into kissing him on Friday?"

"Uh..." This was like that question, *When did you stop beating your wife?* There was no good answer. "He's never threatened me, Trevor. He doesn't scare me."

"I'm here for you," he said. "You know that, right? You can always count on me."

"I know." I turned to him and smiled, even though my stomach was doing flip-flops. "And I appreciate it."

On stage they sang, *"A crazy planet full of crazy people, is somersaulting all around the sky."*

And don't I know it. Stop the world, I want to get off.

They got to the end of their song and started again. I flipped ahead in my script. The next part of the scene was where Mike and I had to kiss. I swallowed hard. Would she make us actually kiss on stage? Would it be as awesome a kiss as at the dance? Could I stand on stage and kiss Mike right in front of my boyfriend. Of course, I'd stood in the middle of the gym and kissed him in front of everyone.

When they were done with this song, I'd have to go back on stage again, and I'd have to kiss Mike. I couldn't do it.

When they'd gone through the song four times, Mrs. Valente looked at her watch and said, "We'll finish this scene tomorrow."

I almost cheered. I'd been reprieved for a day.

Chapter 11
"A Crazy Planet Full of Crazy People"

But the reprieve only lasted until the next day at rehearsal. And now I was going to have to kiss Mike. In front of Trevor. I didn't really see any way out of it.

I was on stage with Mike and we were less than a page away from where it said, "They kiss."

"You should be looking at the Captain, Maria," Mrs. Valente said.

"Uh-huh," I answered, and kept my eyes firmly on the script.

"*I look at you now, and I realize this is not something that has just happened,*" Mike said.

I glanced at him, saw those blue eyes boring into me, and looked away again.

"*That was not just an ordinary dance, was it?*" the Captain asked Maria.

Because of course, when the Captain and Maria danced that folk dance, it had kindled romantic feelings in them. Mike and I had danced and we had kissed. The parallels were spooky.

It was time for the kiss. I braced myself. I wanted to be kissed again like Mike had kissed me at the dance. No. I didn't. Trevor was in the audience watching. Everyone was watching. Did they all know about the kiss at the dance? Were they waiting to see what would happen now? What *would* happen now?

Nothing. He kissed me. But it was nothing like at the dance. It was a quick, gentle peck, and I stepped back, away from him. When I looked at him, his expression was unreadable. Was he holding back because we were being watched, or was that all the kiss he wanted to give me? But I didn't want more. Right?

"You're supposed to be happy about the kiss," Mrs. Valente said.

"Yes. Okay." I stole a glance out to the audience where Trevor was frowning. But what was I supposed to do? It was in the script.

Mrs. Valente just shook her head. "Let's keep going. We'll come back to this scene later."

We sang our song, and I avoided looking at Mike, because whenever I did, I could only think about the kiss at the dance. When he touched, me I stiffened. When he asked who he should ask permission to marry me, I felt like crying. I couldn't do this. I couldn't separate reality from fantasy and do this.

We left the stage together. Out front I could hear Mrs. Valente directing the nuns who had a quick walk-through now. I'd been terrible in that scene and I knew it. I flopped onto the prop sofa and put my head in my hands. I could do better than that.

But not if I had to pretend to be in love with Mike. It just wasn't going to work. I was a good actress, but I wasn't good enough to do this.

I took a deep breath, trying to make the lump in my throat go away.

"You okay?"

The voice was quiet, but it startled me just the same. Mike had sat down next to me.

"Yeah. Fine," I lied.

"That scene was a little rough." He put his hands on his knees, almost like he wanted to make a point of not touching me.

"Sorry about that. It was my fault."

"Yeah."

What was he doing agreeing with me? I turned and glared at him. "Why'd you have to go and kiss me, anyway?"

"It says to—in the script," Mike said, eyebrow raised.

"No." I shook my head and waited for some of the "children" to pass. "I mean at the dance. Why'd you have to do that?"

He didn't answer right away. Finally he shrugged and grinned. "Didn't you like it?"

"That is *so* not the point," I jumped up and put my hands on my hips.

His smile only got bigger. "You're cute when you're angry." He patted the sofa cushion next to him. "Come on, sit back down. I promise not to kiss you."

I sat down. "Well, if you promise." I looked up and saw Sara watching us from a few feet away. I ignored her.

"You're awful jumpy after one kiss, almost a week ago."

I studied the floor boards.

"It's almost like it was a big deal to you."

"It can't be a big deal to me." I forced myself to look him right in the eyes—right in those beautiful, blue eyes. "I have a boyfriend."

Mike nodded. Nuns started to come off stage. Their walk-through scene was over. Mike stood up and reached out a hand to me. "I think that's your cue."

He was right. I was needed back on stage again.

The nuns were getting me ready for my "wedding." I looked off-stage. Mike stood watching me, arms folded. Out in the audience, Trevor had a very similar expression. Why did things have to be so complicated?

Mike came on stage and took my arm as we processed across the stage while the nuns sang, *"How do you solve a problem like Maria?"*

I pulled my arm from his as soon as we were off stage and went to find a secluded corner. This time I actually had a few pages of script before I had to go back on. I squirreled myself away behind a rack of costumes from previous shows and sat down on a box. Mike followed me there.

"I was looking for a little privacy," I pointed out, in case sitting behind the rack of costumes wasn't enough of a clue.

"Privacy's good." Mike sat down on the box next to me. There really wasn't room for both of us on this box. "You know what the problem is?"

"Which problem? The one where I can't act opposite you because you kissed me, or the one where my boyfriend is jealous, or the one where my friends think they know what's best for me or that my sister keeps giving me weird looks or that my brother butts into my life all the time."

"The one where you can't act opposite me," Mike said.

That was supposed to be a rhetorical question. "And I suppose you know why that is?" I snapped. "Well, so do I." I twisted my hand in the fabric of Maria's wedding gown. "It's because you kissed me."

"It's because you want me to kiss you again."

"I do not!" I stood up, but I bumped my head on the clothes rack and sat back down again.

"Are you sure?" He had such a teasing glint in his eye that I wanted to hit him.

"Quite sure," I said as frostily as I could.

He shrugged. "If you're sure." He started to stand up.

"Wait," I said.

He sat back down again.

"What if you're right? If you kissed me again, would I suddenly have no problems acting with you?"

"Let's find out," he said.

"How would that solve our problem?"

He sighed and leaned back. "It wouldn't," he admitted. "But we would know if it was real."

"If what was real?"

"Don't you feel it?" He moved closer to me again. His warm breath stroked my cheeks.

"Feel what?" I asked almost soundlessly. Was he talking about the way my heart raced when we did the folk dance together? Or the way my skin tingled when he was near me? Or was it the way I really wanted him to kiss me again?

"I think you know what I mean, Emma." He reached out and took my hand in his.

I looked at our hands, touching. His hand was warm and gentle. "No. All that means is that we are really good actors."

"No one is that good an actor."

I pulled my hand away. "I am," I insisted, my chin high.

"Are you?" he asked, raising one eyebrow.

And then he slid his arm around me and turned me to face him. He brought his face close to mine. And we kissed again. My arms went around him. And I wasn't acting at all. This kiss was even better than the one at the dance; it felt so right. I didn't want this kiss to end. Ever.

"They're back, they're back!" the children called from the stage.

We pulled apart quickly.

"Whoops, that's our cue," Mike said.

We rushed on to the stage.

I didn't have my script. But I knew my first line. "*Children! Max*!" I said, trying to catch my breath.

Jake had a line, and then Mike. And then they looked at me. My line? What was it? Mike showed me his script. Okay. I was good now.

Mrs. Valente stopped us to move people around a bit and I stole a look at Mike's script to see what my next few lines were.

Deep breath.

We continued with the scene, and then Mike had to exit. He discretely handed me his script before he left, standing just off stage where I could see him. Then Jake left as well, and it was just me and Sara. Maria and Liesl. This was the reprise of "Sixteen Going on Seventeen." I didn't get to be Liesl, but I got to sing the song anyway.

Sara said her line. *"Maria, I've always known you loved us children. Now I know you love Father."*

There was something in her face as she said it. She couldn't know about what happened backstage with Mike, could she? She couldn't. We'd been alone, and it had only been a moment.

But I had a line now. I swallowed hard and tried to be Maria, not Emma. *"I do, Liesl. I love him very much."*

I was talking about the Captain, not Mike. But the feel of Mike's lips on mine made me almost feel weak as I said it.

And then we were into the song. And Mrs. Valente didn't even interrupt us. I was beginning to feel like I was in character again. Maybe I could do this after all. Then Trevor was on stage. It was our one scene together, and I couldn't look him in the eye. He was totally in character, though, being cold to both me and Sara.

"Take a five minute break and we'll resume with the next scene," Mrs. Valente said.

Thank goodness. I needed a break. Lauren was sitting in a seat in the front row and I joined her—she wasn't in most of the second act.

"You're a little off your game today," she commented.

I grabbed a bottle of water out of my backpack and took a drink. "Yeah." It wasn't like I could explain why.

"If you want me to help you with some of your lines sometime, I will."

I sat down next to her. "Would you?"

"Sure."

"Do you think I'm in over my head?" I asked.

She shrugged and tossed her hair over her shoulder. "It's the second week of rehearsal," she said. "Things have to get better from here. And I do think you can do it."

Trevor came over and went through his jacket pockets. He frowned as he checked the last pocket again. "I know it was here," he said, almost to himself.

"What?" I asked.

"Did you lose something?" Lauren asked.

"My iPod. I was going to play something for Sara, but I can't find it."

"You sure you had it?" I bent to look under the seats. Perhaps it had fallen.

"I'm sure."

Sara joined us then, and started looking. "Did it have any distinguishing features?" she asked.

Good point. One iPod could look much like another.

"Besides my play list? It was in the black case Emma gave me for Christmas." Trevor joined me in looking under the seats. "I don't understand where it could have gotten to," he muttered. "I had it at lunch, right? You saw it."

"I saw it," I assured. "Did you look in your backpack?"

"Not there."

"Maybe someone stole it," Sara said, as she looked in and around the seats near Trevor's stuff.

"Who would do that?" I asked. The only people here were people in the play.

"You never know." Sara was digging in my coat pockets now.

"Why are you looking in my coat?"

"Maybe he loaned it to you, but he forgot."

"*I* wouldn't forget though. He didn't lend it to me."

"Whatever." Sara shrugged and continued digging in other people's stuff. "Hey, is this it?" she asked, suddenly.

I looked up. She was standing near Mike's jacket and holding a black-cased iPod. Trevor rushed over to her. "Yeah. This sure looks like it." He turned it on and checked the playlist. "Where did you find it?"

"The pocket of Mike's jacket."

Mike had taken Trevor's iPod?

Mike was sitting on the edge of the stage. We all turned to face him.

"What's my iPod doing in your jacket?" Trevor asked, his voice low and steady.

"Beats me." Mike looked unfazed and a little annoyed. "What are *you* doing in my jacket?"

"Finding my belongings."

"I didn't put it there."

"How else did it get there?" Trevor's voice rose and he took a step toward Mike.

"Why would I take your stuff?" Mike didn't move from his perch on the edge of the stage.

"How should I know?"

"Besides, I've been on stage all afternoon. When would I have time to steal something from you, assuming I would want to?"

"You weren't on stage the whole time," Sara pointed out.

Mike looked directly at me.

Right. When he wasn't on stage he was backstage with me, or I'd been watching him, standing in the wings. And then of course there was the time we were both backstage, kissing. He couldn't have taken anything.

Did he expect me to tell everyone that I'd been kissing him backstage? I couldn't do that. I turned away and said nothing.

"Charges of theft are very serious," Mrs. Valente said.

"I didn't steal anything," Mike said, his voice rising in frustration.

"Prove it," Trevor challenged.

"Prove I did it." Mike jumped off the stage and advanced toward Trevor, his fists clenched.

"He's going to hit him," someone said.

Mike took a step back.

"My iPod was in your jacket pocket," Trevor said as if that was all there was to say.

"I didn't put it there," Mike insisted.

"Then how did it get there?" Trevor asked.

"Hey, I don't know."

Mrs. Valente took charge. "Does anyone know how Trevor's iPod got into Mike's jacket?" she asked.

No one answered.

Mrs. Valente looked at her watch. "I want you all to go home and think about what you know. Someone obviously knows what was going on. We can't have people stealing from each other."

So that was it, the end of rehearsal for today.

Mike could say he'd been with me and that would be the end of it. I could say he was with me, and that would be that. But neither of us said anything. I knew why I didn't say anything. I didn't know why Mike didn't say anything.

Mike just gathered up his stuff and left, not even looking at me. Why did it feel like there was a rock in the bottom of my stomach?

"Figures."

"Never should have let him in the play."

"Always thought he looked like a hoodlum."

Comments drifted past me as I put on my coat. But Mike wasn't a hoodlum. He was a nice guy. And he didn't take that iPod.

Chapter 12
"To Laugh and Weep Together"

"It was only a matter of time before Anderson showed his true colors," Trevor said, dipping his nacho into the salsa as we sat in a booth at the Snack Shack.

"Maybe now he'll get kicked out of the play," Sara said and took a long, thoughtful sip of her soda.

"And not a moment too soon." Lauren leaned against Jake. "They should just kick him out of school and be done with it."

Caitlyn picked up a nacho and then held it poised over the salsa. "I don't know," she said, "he never seemed to be in trouble or anything since he got here."

Lauren nudged Caitlyn's nacho out of the way so she could dip hers. "He's bringing the whole image of St. Stephen's down."

Mike had said the kids at St. Stephen's were snobs. I ran my finger over the condensation on my glass. Maybe he was right.

"You're awfully quiet, Emma." Trevor put his arm around me. "Probably can't believe that the underdog really does deserve to be on the bottom, huh?"

"I just think you guys are judging him too quickly," I said.

Jake laughed. "Em, the iPod was in his jacket. How much more proof do you want?" He picked up a nacho and waved it at me, as if waving a pointer. "The problem you have is that you're being swayed by the character he plays. He's only the up-standing Captain on stage. The rest of the time he's still the same old Biker Mike."

"Just 'cause he rides a motorcycle doesn't mean he'd steal something."

"The iPod was in his pocket," Sara said as if that sealed the deal.

It was true. The only clue pointed to him, but it couldn't have been him. He had an iron-clad alibi: me. Trevor's arm felt heavy on my shoulders, like a yoke that was preventing me from telling them what had happened backstage.

"Let's not talk about him anymore," Caitlyn said, in her usual upbeat way. "Can you believe they voted Clarissa off of *American Beauties* last night?"

"I'm not going to sit here and talk about *American Beauties*," Jake said. "Everyone knows the most important thing that was on TV last night was the Devils' game."

So the conversation veered off into things that had nothing to do with Mike and the play, and I was able to relax a little, knowing I wouldn't spill my secret if we were talking about the hockey game.

The next morning I spun the lock on my locker with foolish confidence. Of course, it didn't open. Not on the first try, or the second try, or the third try. All around me people were opening their lockers, getting things out, closing them again, and going on their way. I stood there like a fool in front of my stupid locker. I glanced to my right, where Mike's locker was. He wasn't there. This was a day when I'd appreciate it if he offered to help.

I tried again, and just as I got to the last number, someone covered my eyes with his hands. "Guess who?"

Trevor. Obviously. "Hey! I was just about to get my locker open."

He uncovered my eyes. "Not a very warm greeting." He leaned against the locker next to mine.

I sighed and shoved away my impatience. "Sorry, but you know the trouble my locker gives me." I turned the dial one more time and this time it opened.

"You should probably ask for a new locker," Trevor said.

The thought had occurred to me.

"One that's not so close to Anderson's."

Of course, that hadn't been my reason. "Trust me, he's not going to steal anything from my locker," I said. "No one can even get it open."

"You can't be too careful," Trevor said.

I closed my locker and we started walking down the hall to homeroom.

"So, what movie do you want to see tonight?"

"Can we do something else?" I asked.

"We always go to the movies," Trevor said.

"Kind of my point. Can't we do something else? Like bowling or something?"

"Bowling?"

"I don't know. Just something different."

"We could go to the Snack Shack?" Trevor suggested.

"And how exactly is that different?" We got to homeroom. I sat in my seat, while Trevor stood next to me.

"Roller skating?" Trevor finally suggested.

I smiled. "Now that could be cool."

The late bell rang and Trevor went to his seat.

That afternoon Mrs. Valente started the rehearsal with a lecture about values and proper behavior and the morals that are implicit with attending a Catholic school. I watched Mike, sitting in the second row back, his jaw clenched, staring straight ahead.

"Since there is no proof that Mike took the iPod—" Mrs. Valente started.

"It was in his jacket," Trevor shouted out.

"That doesn't mean he put it there," Mrs. Valente said calmly. "And, since the item was returned to its owner, we will drop this matter. But I expect, in the future, to see only behavior befitting St. Stephen's students from all of you."

And with that we got to work. I was glad Mike wasn't going to get in trouble for something he didn't do.

I got on stage with him and the other children—we were supposed to be singing at the Salzburg Music Festival.

"I'm glad it all worked out," I said to Mike. And I hadn't even had to let Trevor know I'd been kissing someone else.

"No thanks to you," he said, his voice icy. He turned from me to get ready to start the scene.

Okay, I guess I deserved that.

It was hard to do the scenes—where we were supposed to be a happy, newly-married couple, taking on the world together—when every time he looked at me a chill went down my spine because his eyes were so stone cold.

We finished up. It was with great relief that I closed my script on the last line of the play. It had only taken us two weeks. We'd better get faster at it; no audience was going to have that much patience.

Mrs. Valente had us start over again from scene one. Luckily—although scene one was short—I wasn't in it. A brief reprieve. I sought out Trevor in the audience and sat next to him.

"I can't believe they didn't kick him out of the play," he said, casting dark looks in Mike's direction.

"What's the big deal? You don't know he took it. Someone could have planted it in his pocket or something."

"This isn't some TV show. No one planted the iPod in his pocket. He took it. He got away with it."

"Got away with what? You have your iPod."

"Emma," Mrs. Valente was calling from the front of the theater. "It's your scene. Get up here."

If only people could see they weren't being fair to Mike. If only I could let them know that without implicating myself. I wasn't really in the mood to sing upbeat and cheery songs right now. But that's what being an actress was all about, right? Being able to step outside myself and become someone else.

Deep breath. How was it Mrs. Valente wanted me to sit? I remembered. Sitting on the floor, leaning on my elbows, one leg balanced on my knee. Luckily I didn't have to stay like this for long, because it wasn't terribly comfortable.

"Anytime you're ready, Emma," Mrs. Valente said.

Right. I needed to start. I gave a nod and the piano accompaniment began. One more deep breath and I began singing, "*My day in the hills has come to an end I know.*" I sat up now and continued, "*A star has come out to tell me it's time to go.*" I could do this. My voice got stronger as I went on.

My song ended and I left the stage. I pretended I was still Maria as I hung out backstage and waited for my cue. It was easier than being me right now. When we finished the scene, Mrs. Valente dismissed us.

"From now on, you will only be required to attend if you are in a scene we're working on that day. A schedule will be posted on the theater door starting Monday."

When I begged out of going to the Snack Shack that afternoon, Trevor looked hurt.

"It's not that I don't want to be with you," I said. What I didn't want was to be surrounded by people who were saying bad things about Mike. I just wasn't in the mood for that. I smiled at Trevor. "And I'll see you tonight. This way I can get some homework done first."

It was pleasantly mild as I walked home by myself. Normally, I would have liked the time to think my own thoughts. Right now, I didn't really like where those thoughts were leading me. I just went over my lines as I walked. When I got home, I actually did work on my homework. One thing about having the lead, it took a lot of time. Last year I'd been able to work on homework at rehearsals, not this year.

I was just finishing up my math problems when Jake came into my room.

"Don't you ever knock?" I asked as I put my math notebook away.

"Nope. As the big brother, that's my prerogative."

"As the little sister, I say you better start giving me privacy."

"Whatever." He sat down on my bed. "You were good today."

"Thanks." I tucked my trig book into my backpack.

"You sucked yesterday." That was just like Jake: brutally honest.

"Thanks. You can leave now."

"What's up with you and Mike? You were kissing him at the dance, but now you can't seem to be near him."

"I wasn't kissing him at the dance," I said.

Jake just glanced over at me, one eyebrow cocked.

"Okay, we kissed."

"You two have to be able to be on stage together, so you better get your issues worked out."

I hated when Jake pulled his big brother act on me. I hated even more that he was right: Mike and I *were* going to have to be able to work together. I'd have to figure out a way to fix things with Mike, without messing things up with Trevor.

****

"I'm not sure why I agreed to come here," Trevor said as he fastened his in-line skates.

"You didn't agree," I reminded him, "you suggested it."

"It was better than *bowling*," he said with

disdain. "You don't know who you might run into at a bowling alley. Bikers go there."

Had Trevor always been such a snob?

I tightened my skates and stood up, slightly wobbly at first. I hadn't been to the rink since last summer, when Caitlyn had her birthday party here. Trevor took my hand and led me to the polished wood floor. The DJ had the music cranked up and the disco ball over the rink made everything sparkle.

As we skated to the music, I realized that this was a lot like dancing: feeling the beat, moving with it. Maybe I could get Trevor to take me here more often. At first we skated side by side, and then Trevor decided to skate backwards, but a rink employee told him he couldn't: too dangerous to the other skaters.

"I'm ready for a break anyway," Trevor said.

So we got off the rink and headed to the arcade games. There were lots of video games and games of chance—and one pinball game.

"Did I ever tell you that I'm a pinball wizard?" Trevor said, heading straight for the pinging blinking machine.

"You never mentioned that."

"I am." He stopped to get tokens and fed them into the game. I watched as he played, saving the ball every time before it fell into the gap.

"Hey, Mike's friend!" I heard a little girl say.

I turned to see Mike's little sister, the older one. Was she Julie or Madeline? Her ponytails looked like floppy black rabbit ears on top of her head. She was holding her mother's hand.

"Oh, hi," I said, as the ball Trevor had kept going all this time was lost.

"Hi, Emma," Mike's mom said cheerfully. "Nice to see you again."

Trevor turned from his game and put his arm possessively around my shoulder.

"It's nice to see you too," I said. Was Mike here?

Or was it just his mom and the little girls?

"You gonna come play with us again?" the little girl asked.

I could feel Trevor tense next to me.

"I don't know," I answered. Then, counting on the fact that preschoolers have notoriously short attention spans, I changed the subject. "Do you like to roller skate?" She was wearing the kiddie skates, the kind where the wheels only moved forward.

"I falls down lots," she said matter-of-factly.

Her mother smiled. "Come along, Madeline, let's leave Emma alone now."

They moved on, but not before Madeline gave me one more big smile and said, "Bye, Mike's friend."

Trevor turned around and pulled the lever to start the next ball going. "So, who was that?" he asked, as he leaned into the machine.

"Mike's mom and little sister."

"You've been hanging out at Mike's house?" He banged the buttons on the side.

"I was over there once." I said, trying to sound nonchalant and casual about it.

He leaned on the machine some more and banged the buttons. Finally he said, "So, how long have you been seeing him?"

"Seeing him? I see him every day at rehearsal. That's as far as it goes."

Trevor grunted something and then said, "You went to his house."

"Yeah." I took a step back from the pinball game. "I was under the impression I was your girlfriend, not your possession."

The ball dropped again and he turned to me. "I think you just want to be with whoever you're spending the most time in a play with. Last year it was me. Now it's Mike."

"I never said I wanted to spend more time with Mike and less with you."

"And you keep defending him," Trevor

continued, ignoring the fact that I'd spoken.

"He didn't take the iPod."

"No kidding he didn't take it," Trevor said, "but it would have been the perfect way to get him out of the play—and out of our lives."

No kidding he didn't take it? "What do you know about the iPod going missing?"

"I know it was missing and found in Mike's jacket." He pulled the lever on the pinball game for his last ball.

"And that's all?" I leaned over the game so he'd have to see me.

"That's all."

He was totally lying. "Did you set him up?"

The last ball went straight into the hole. Game Over.

"What's it to you?" Trevor asked, turning to face me and crossing his arms.

"You can't just try to get people in trouble. It's not nice." I said, and even as I said it, it sounded really lame.

"I told you, I didn't set him up," Trevor repeated. "How come when Mike says something you believe him, but when I do, you doubt me?"

Because I knew Mike was telling the truth. But I didn't think it would be wise to point that out.

"You don't even have a good answer," Trevor said. He shook his head and sighed. "I'm going to call my mom to take me home. You can find your own ride. Maybe Mike will bring you home on his motorcycle."

Had I just heard him right? "You're just going to leave me here?"

"Yeah," he said and headed toward the lockers. My shoes and jacket were in the same locker as his so I followed him, skating around little kids and big kids and parents watching from the sidelines.

"You know what I think?" I asked when I managed to catch up with him. "I think this has nothing to do with Mike. I think you're the one who likes to date the person you are spending time on stage with. Will you be asking Sara out next?"

He hesitated a second too long before answering. "This has nothing to do with Sara."

He handed me my coat and my shoes. I stuck them back in the locker. "Just give me the key. I'm not leaving yet."

"What are you going to do?" he asked as he took off his skates.

"I'm going to skate. That's why I came here."

"Rendezvous with Mike you mean?" he asked.

"Do you know how stupid you sound? You asked me to go roller skating. Why would I ask someone else to meet me here? It's not like I knew you were going to break up with me during the middle of our date."

"I see you don't deny that you wouldn't mind seeing him here."

"You're an idiot," I said with a shake of my head.

When Trevor's mom got there, she insisted I call my mom while she was watching so she knew I had a ride home. Once she was satisfied, I headed back to the wooden skate floor. I skated as fast as I could without bumping into other people, or being stopped for being a daredevil. I couldn't believe he just broke up with me in the middle of a date. And why? Because I knew Mike's little sister? How incredibly jealous was that?

It was on my fourth or fifth time around the rink that I noticed him, standing outside the skating area, leaning against the wall and watching, still wearing that leather jacket.

He had said we had feelings for each other, and I'd tried to deny them. Maybe it was time to stop denying and get things straightened out between us. After all, as Jake pointed out, we needed to work our issues out if we were going to be on stage together.

I left the rink and skated up to where he was

standing. "Hi," I said.

Mike turned and looked at me coolly, then turned his attention back to the skaters.

That's okay. I would just forge ahead anyway. "I've been doing some thinking," I said brightly.

"Yeah?" he said, as casually as if I were about to give him the weather report.

"Yeah." I took a deep breath. "About what you said the other day—about us maybe having feelings for each other…and I think…"

Mike put up his hand to stop me. "I was wrong."

"What?" This was not the turn of events I was expecting.

"Just that," Mike said, his voice low and even. "You're not the kind of person I thought you were."

"What kind of person did you think I was?" My head was starting to hurt. "Did you think I was some sort of a Biker Chick? Did you think I was easy or something?"

Mike finally looked at me. There was no friendliness in his eyes. "You think girls who ride motorcycles are 'easy'?"

"No," I backtracked. "That's not what I meant. But I want to know what you mean."

Mike sighed and said, "I thought you were nice."

"I *am* nice," I said instantly.

"A nice person would have stood up for me, not let everyone think the worst about me. You're all about image. You're just concerned with what people think about you." Mike turned away from me, as if to say the conversation was over.

"But…" With a sinking feeling I realized he might be right. "I'm sorry," I murmured and skated away.

How had I managed to screw so much up in so short a time?

Chapter 13
"A Bell is No Bell till You Ring It"

"Want to talk about it?" Mom asked as we drove away from the roller rink.

"No." I stared out the window at the brown piles of leftover snow, illuminated by the street lights. I was ready for spring.

Mom didn't press but obviously she knew something was wrong. Otherwise why would she be picking me up from my date? The house was quiet when we got home. Sara and Jake were both still out having successful social lives. Dad was at a Rotary meeting or something. I flopped down on the family room couch and flipped through the TV channels. *Casablanca* was playing on one of the movie channels. Maybe a good old-fashioned romance would teach me how things were supposed to be done.

A few minutes later, Mom came into the room carrying a tray with a bowl of popcorn and two glasses of soda. I moved the *Sports Illustrated*, *TV Guide,* and *Seventeen* out of the way so she could put it down on the coffee table.

We watched in silence for awhile, and then when Humphrey Bogart was remembering how Ilsa had left him at the train station I said, "Trevor and I broke up."

"Ah," she said and took a handful of popcorn. "I had wondered."

"He wasn't as perfect for me as I thought," I explained.

"I see," she said.

"Well, anyway. It's over."

"I'm sorry."

"Aren't you going to tell me there are plenty of other fish in the sea?" Wasn't that the kind of thing mothers were supposed to say?

"There are," she answered with a thoughtful nod. "But I don't suppose you feel much like fishing right now."

Except Mike; I could "fish" for Mike. Only he hated me. I sighed.

"You know," Mom said.

Oh great: a lecture. I knew one had to be on the way.

"There was a time when I thought I was never going to find true love."

"That was before you met Dad, right?" Of course it was. Because I'm sure that as soon as she met Dad they knew right away that they were destined for each other. That was how it worked.

"No," Mom said.

I waited for more, but she didn't seem inclined to continue. "Well?" I prompted.

She smiled at me. "We didn't seem like such a good fit at the beginning, that's all."

"You and Dad? But you're perfect together." How could they have ever not seemed right for each other?

"Things have a funny way of working out in the end." Mom patted my knee. Maybe there was hope for my life after all? "They even worked out for Bogie." She turned her attention to the TV.

"Doesn't the girl leave with someone else in this movie?" I asked.

"Well, romance-wise, no, this movie isn't the best for him, that's true. Maybe that wasn't a good example."

"Yeah, maybe not."

We watched for a while in silence. "Mom?" I said, not looking at her, but taking a few pieces of popcorn out of the bowl.

"Yes?"

"If you've really screwed something up, is it possible to make it better?"

"Care to share details?" Mom asked.

"No."

"Okay, then. If you're supposed to cut a board to six feet six inches and you cut it to just six feet, you can't make it long again."

"That doesn't help me."

"I need to know what you screwed up," she said and gave me a little smile.

I didn't want to tell her everything. But I did, bit by bit till she had the whole story out of me. "Can I fix it?"

"Which part do you want to fix? The part with Trevor or Mike?"

"I don't think I can fix things with Trevor. And, honestly, I'm not sure I want to."

"As far as Mike goes, you need to come clean, with everyone."

"That will be hard."

"I never said fixing things was easy."

Right. We watched the rest of the movie in silence, but I caught Mom stealing glances at me from time to time. Had I been right to tell her everything?

****

"*High on a hill was a lonely goatherd,*" I sang Monday afternoon. Singing was good. It helped me to forget everything else. It helped me forget that Trevor, who used to walk me to all my classes and sit with me at lunch, hadn't looked my way once today. It helped me to forget the weird conversation I had in the hall with some girl I barely knew who said how sorry she was that Trevor and I had broken up, because it spelled doom for all relationships since we couldn't make it work and we were the perfect couple. "Looks can be deceiving," I'd said over the lump in my throat.

But now I was on stage and I was yodeling my heart out. Everything else could be forgotten. Almost.

My song over, I left the stage. "Good singing," Lauren said when I encountered her backstage, waiting to go on.

"Thanks." I was still catching my breath. Yodeling was hard work.

"You might want to stay clear of Trevor."

Suddenly everything came crashing back on me. I'd been staying clear of Trevor. Or rather, he'd been doing a heck of a job staying clear of me. I swallowed hard. "Why?" I wasn't sure I wanted to know the answer, but I had to ask.

Lauren shrugged. "He's just mouthing off some."

Great, he broke up with me and now he's going to badmouth me too? Why had I ever thought he was such a great boyfriend?

I had a while before my next cue, but I decided to heed Lauren's advice and steer clear of Trevor, so I stayed backstage, settling onto the sofa. Maybe I should go and confront Trevor. Maybe that would make more sense than sitting back here hiding from him. But then, if he was saying nasty stuff, I really didn't want to hear it.

The "servants" came off stage, walking past the sofa I sat on.

"They should just kick him out of the play," the girl who played the maid said to the boy who played the butler.

"I know. I leave everything in my locker now, I don't want anything to go missing," the boy said.

"I heard that he was kicked out of his last school for stealing."

"Maybe they should kick him out of here."

"As Sister Patricia would say: 'he's not an asset to the St. Stephen's community.'"

They left the backstage area, their parts done for now. Were they talking about Mike? That wasn't fair. Mike hadn't taken the iPod. But everyone thought he did. And if I didn't step forward and tell what I knew, they would keep talking about him that way. And Mike would be right about me. I wasn't very nice.

But if I did tell, then I'd be admitting to kissing Mike while still dating Trevor. I didn't want people to think I was the kind of person who cheats on a boyfriend. Because I don't. At least not intentionally.

Mike was on stage with Lauren now. The Captain was telling Elsa that she was fun to be with, quite an experience for him. I guess that was true enough. Lauren could certainly be an "experience."

She answered, "*You're quite an experience for me, too. Somewhere in you there's a fascinating man. Occasionally I catch a glimpse of him, and when I do, he's exciting.*"

I caught my breath. That was almost like she was reading my mind. I'd seen glimpses of a fascinating person behind the leather coat and long hair. I wanted to get to know him better. And I'd completely ruined my chance. My eyes burned with unshed tears. I blinked them away.

Someone plopped himself down on the sofa next to me. "My, aren't Mike and Lauren looking mighty cozy out there," Jake said.

"They're supposed to," I answered.

"True enough. Are you hiding from Trevor?"

"Should I be?" Maybe staying back here wasn't the best idea. Maybe I should have confronted him as soon as I got off stage. Did people think I was hiding? Was I? Did I care?

"If I were you, I wouldn't want to be hanging out near him," was all Jake would say.

Oh, very nice. Very comforting.

Jake stood. "Time for me to go break up that cozy duo." He headed on stage.

Shortly, Mike had to exit. My heart beat faster as he walked right to where I was sitting. But he didn't look at me. Instead he turned and faced the stage. He stood mere feet from me, but didn't look at me. I wanted him to look at me. I would go to him. I would tell him I was sorry. I could fix this. I knew I could.

I stood up, but as I reached him, he walked back onto the stage. I stood in the wings and watched Lauren and Jake sing. Last time they'd sung this at rehearsal I'd been snuggled against Trevor. How quickly everything had changed.

"You're not as great as you think you are," Trevor said, suddenly at my side.

"What?" I asked, startled. But he was already on stage. Was that the kind of stuff he'd been saying out front? Oh, what did it matter anyway? He'd broken up with me, who cared what he thought?

The "children" were gathering backstage, getting ready for our entrance. I took a deep breath and tried to put myself back in character. Lauren and Jake both exited, and then the children began leapfrogging onto the stage.

I went last and ended at Mike's feet. Last time we'd done this scene he'd smiled indulgently at me. I was hoping for a similar reaction. I stood up and said my line. Mike barely looked at me. He was perfectly in character as the stern captain.

Why was he so mad at me? So, I hadn't spoken up. But he could have said something too. I probably wouldn't have denied it.

The Captain complained about the play clothes the children wore. He made them wear sailor suits all the time, Maria argued back. Maria was angry.

It was easy to act angry with him because he hadn't been treating me fairly. I felt Maria's righteous anger and I used it. "*You're not home long enough to know them.*"

"*I said I don't want to hear—*"

"Of course you don't," I answered, no longer in the part of Maria. "You don't even give a person a chance to explain."

"And what is there to explain?" Mike fired back.

"Like how it isn't all my fault," I answered, taking a step toward him and looking into those eyes. He had to look at me now.

"I never said anything was your fault," he replied, and his eyes were stone cold when he said it.

"You sure act like it," I said, putting one hand on my hip.

"Captain, Maria—I think we've strayed from the script," Mrs. Valente said.

Right. The script. "Oh, sorry," I said, and taking a step back, looked at the script I was holding. Right now Maria had to argue with the Captain. If I were going to argue with Mike it would have to happen later. If he'd let me talk to him.

We muddled through the rest of the scene and finally rehearsal was over. I was glad. I just wanted to get home.

"Maybe we should pat him down before he leaves, make sure he's not sneaking out with anything," the boy who played Franz said.

I looked up and saw that Mike had heard the remark. His shoulders sagged slightly, before he turned and started walking slowly toward the exit. It wasn't fair. Mike hadn't done anything. And I could prove it. I jumped up on stage and grabbed the microphone.

"Hey. Wait a minute everyone," I said.

People stopped what they were doing and turned to look at me. Even Mike. Even Trevor. I was burning my bridges now. I took a deep breath. "Mike Anderson did not take Trevor McGrath's iPod."

"Prove it," someone shouted.

"I can," I said. "Because during the time when he wasn't on stage that day—the only time he wasn't on stage and would have had time to steal something—if indeed he were the kind of person to steal something—which he's not—he was backstage with me."

"Why didn't you say something before?" someone asked.

"Because," I might as well go for broke, "we were making out, and I didn't want my boyfriend to know."

There. I'd said it all.

"What a slut," someone said. I think it was Trevor, and the words hit me like a punch in the stomach. I took a breath to respond, but I didn't know what to say. Was Trevor right? Is that the label that would be affixed to me now, just because I had kissed Mike? Kissed. That's all we'd done. I looked for Mike but he wasn't anywhere to be seen.

Jake came to the base of the stage. "Come on down, Emma. Let's go home."

I turned the microphone off. "I just wanted people to stop treating Mike like a leper or something. It's not fair. He didn't do anything."

Mrs. Valente walked over as I jumped down from the stage. "You shouldn't have kept that information to yourself, Emma," she said, frowning.

"It seemed kind of private," I said. Why had Mike left? He was supposed to forgive me now. Nothing was working out like it was supposed to.

"We have certain standards we expect St. Stephen's students to adhere to," Mrs. Valente said.

I looked at her. "But I came clean. I did my bit. Now make people be nice to Mike."

Mrs. Valente smiled sadly. "I can't make people be nice to other people."

I wanted to say, "Then what good are you?" but I simply rolled my eyes instead and Mrs. Valente walked off.

Sara was right there, waiting to speak as soon as the coast was clear. "You were making out with Mike backstage?" She crossed her arms and tapped her foot, looking for all the world like a disapproving parent.

"Just that once," I said. Once and only once, probably.

"Let's go home," Jake repeated.

I had done the right thing. I knew I had. Shouldn't I feel better about it? Shouldn't I be basking in the glow of righteousness? Why did I just feel like a huge loser?

"That was a really stupid thing you did," Lauren said from the front seat as we drove home.

"Totally," Sara agreed.

"Shouldn't I have told the truth?"

Lauren turned to face me. "The first stupid thing you did was kiss him. The second stupid thing you did was tell everyone."

"I couldn't let him take the heat for something he didn't do," I insisted.

"Why not?" Lauren said. "He was bound to do something to mess up before the play, better to have him out early when it will be easier to replace him, than later."

"Who says he's going to mess stuff up. He's good. He played Lancelot in *Camelot* last year. He wasn't kicked out of any schools. His stepdad was just transferred."

"I think you know a little bit too much about him," Lauren said with a raised eyebrow.

"I don't think you know him at all."

"Precisely."

Jake pulled into the driveway and Sara and I got out. Apparently Jake and Lauren weren't staying though, because they took off again.

"Did you have to go start hanging out with losers?" Sara asked. "That makes it so much harder for me."

"It's not all about you, Sara," I said as I unlocked the front door.

"It's not all about you either!" She headed up to her room.

I went into the kitchen and got a snack. Things

would look better after a good night's sleep. That's what Mom always said. I had to believe that was true.

But things didn't look any better the next day. As I struggled with my locker, I heard some girls whispering to each other as they passed me.

"Can you believe she cheated on Trevor with Biker Mike?"

I turned to see who it was, but they had already faded into the morning rush. What got me, though, was the way they said Trevor's name, so reverently, and practically spat out Mike's name. What did they know about any of it? Trevor was no angel, and Mike wasn't evil incarnate. If there was one thing I'd learned from this whole Trevor/Mike mess it was that people shouldn't just judge by first appearances.

If Mike would just stop by my locker, then everything would be all right. I'd know that he'd forgiven me. I'd know that he'd accepted my publicly clearing his name as an apology and we could move forward. I saw him at his locker, only a few feet away, but he didn't make a move toward mine, didn't even look in my direction.

Why wait for him? I could go to him, tell him I was really sorry about everything. I'd already abandoned all hope of saving face when I made the announcement from the stage, what did a little more humiliation matter? I gave up trying to open my locker in order to go to him. I didn't know what I was going to say, but I had to say something.

But as I neared, I heard someone say, "Some pair they picked for the leads in the play. He steals and she cheats."

Mike turned to see who had spoken and saw me, but quickly looked away.

I went back to my locker. I couldn't talk to him yet. I had tried to make things better, but I'd only made them worse. I heard other whispered conversations throughout the day like: "Why was she kissing him?" "She never struck me as the kind to cheat." "Just goes to show you can't always tell." "But how did Trevor's iPod end up in Mike's jacket?"

That last question was bothering me too. After all, it hadn't walked there on its own. Someone had put it there. But who? And why?

I knew it wasn't Mike. Trevor had said he hadn't set Mike up, but I couldn't shake the feeling that wasn't true. I wish I could prove it. If I could find out who'd taken the iPod maybe we could get past this whole mess. But I was no Nancy Drew. I wasn't going to be tracking down obscure clues. It would just have to stay a mystery.

I wasn't expecting Trevor to stop by my locker before lunch. I realized those days were over for good, but I was expecting Lauren and Caitlyn. When the halls cleared and they still hadn't come, I headed to the lunchroom by myself. They weren't at our usual table.

I sat down and started to eat. I inched my chair closer to some other juniors sitting at the other end of the table so I wouldn't look quite so alone.

Normally Lauren and I walk to Trig together from lunch, but since she wasn't at lunch, I walked alone. She was already in the classroom when I got there. I stopped by her desk. "Where were you?"

"When?" she pushed her hair behind her ear.

"Lunch."

"Oh. We have standards to maintain, you know," she said.

"Standards? I'm your best friend. I don't meet your standards now?"

The bell rang. "Emma, take your seat," the teacher said.

I took an empty one near the back of the classroom because I didn't want to be too near Lauren right now.

When I got to rehearsal I had to go almost immediately backstage. That was fine, because it kept me from having to talk to anyone. Not that anyone seemed too inclined to talk to me. We were practicing the party scene today. I waited in the wings, with the boy who played Kurt, for my cue. I was going to have to dance with Mike. He was already on stage. He hadn't talked to me yet. He hadn't stopped by my locker. He hadn't said anything to me before rehearsal.

And then I was on stage, explaining to young Kurt that I hadn't danced the *Laendler* in a long time. He convinced me to try to remember. We began dancing and then it was time for Mike to break in.

I tried to get some idea of how he felt by his expression. But he was unreadable. He was simply being the Captain. We continued the dance. I liked dancing with him. Now, holding hands, I had to turn and go under Mike's arms, and then be in his arms, his face close to mine. We were so close. I could feel his warm breath on my cheek. I wanted those lips on mine again. Would I ever get that chance?

I broke away from him. It was in the script. I was supposed to. But I had to anyway because I couldn't be that close to him and not know what he was thinking.

I said my line, my heart beating too fast, stammering, my face flushed, but it all worked because Maria was supposed to be flustered. Mike had to leave the stage then and Lauren came in. The magic was broken. The one thing I knew for certain was that I wanted Mike to forgive me. We had to have another chance.

The scene continued. Mike and I were hardly ever in the same place at the same time. It seemed if I was on stage he was in the wings. If I was waiting for a cue, he was on stage. There was no chance to talk. No chance to get anything straightened out.

We finished and—typical Mrs. Valente—we started again.

Every time we danced, those same butterflies

were in my stomach. I had that same urge to kiss him again, that same desire to always be close to him. But I never got any idea if he felt the same way.

Rehearsal ended for the day. Mike grabbed his stuff and left. I watched him go with a sinking feeling. This was not how things were supposed to happen. In the play when Maria comes back to face the Captain they end up married. I'd gone out on a limb for Mike and I ended up losing all my friends. Life just wasn't fair.

Chapter 14
"Bloom and Grow Forever"

I had to finish reading *Jane Eyre*. That, of course, would keep me from focusing on my other problems. Mainly, my whole life. When I tried to IM Caitlyn, she didn't answer. Lauren didn't return my text messages and neither of them answered their phone.

It appeared that I was currently friendless.

My regular friends wouldn't talk to me because of Mike. And Mike wouldn't talk to me either. I put *Jane Eyre* down. When I'd first gotten the role of Maria, Mike had called to congratulate me. I could call him. I checked the caller id on the phone for his number, but Dad, in his "must keep things organized and neat" way had deleted all the past calls. So, I'd use the phone book—or look him up online.

But there were lots of Andersons in the phone book and I didn't know his dad's first name. Then I realized it was his stepdad. I didn't even know his dad's last name. So much for that idea.

The phone rang and I jumped. Was it some kind of cosmic karma? Had Mike known I was thinking about him and called me? How cool was that? I picked up the phone without even looking at the caller idea.

"Hello," I said.

"Oh, Emma." It was Trevor and he sounded disappointed that I'd answered. Well, he'd called my house, who did he think would answer? "Is Sara there?"

"Sara?" I repeated. A lump the size of a grapefruit settled in the pit of my stomach.

"Um, yeah. I want to talk to her about our parts."

"I'll get her," I said.

When I found her she took the cordless phone and went off to the privacy of her room. All I heard was "Hi, Trev," before she was out of earshot.

Hi, Trev? She was being awfully familiar with my boyfriend. Ex-boyfriend. Whatever.

Not surprisingly the next day none of my friends stopped by my locker. But that didn't mean I had to be a loner. I looked around. A few lockers down from me, in the opposite direction of Mike's locker, was Sami. She was in the play and my homeroom. I didn't know her that well, she was pretty quiet. But that didn't mean I couldn't stop by and say hi. So I did.

She looked startled that I had spoken to her, and pushed her unruly hair behind her ears.

"I just wanted to let you know you're doing a really great job as Sister Sophia," I said.

Sami smiled. "Thanks. Someday I want to be on Broadway."

"Me too!" I said. "We can star in a show together! That would be awesome. And then we could say—when we win our joint Tony award—that we've known each other since those dear old days at St. Stephen's High School."

Sami laughed. She closed her locker and we headed to homeroom. I walked right by Lauren and didn't even look at her.

At lunch I sat with Sami and some of her friends. One of the girls looked up from her ham and cheese sandwich and said, "Isn't it weird, having Mike Anderson play the Captain? He's kind of…."

"He's nice," I said.

Judging by the looks the other girls gave me, I don't think they believed me.

"I was at his house one time," I started to say.

"I heard he lives in a crack house," someone

said.

I laughed. “No. He lives in a center hall colonial over on Oak. He’s got two little sisters and two little brothers and he’s really nice to them. He gives the little girls piggy back rides.”

“What’s with the tattoos and the motorcycle?”

“His dad is really into motorcycles. When it’s his weekend, his dad helps him fix up his bike. It’s a historic motorcycle—from World War II.”

“His weekend,” Sami said, with a nod. “So, he’s from a broken home. That explains it.”

I looked around at the other girls at the table. Mandy, the one with the ham sandwich, had divorced parents too.

“I bet nearly half the student body of St. Stephen’s comes from a broken home,” I said.

Mandy nodded in agreement.

“He does seem to be a pretty good actor,” Sami conceded.

“He’s awesome.” He might not like me anymore, but I’d do what I could to get people to like him. “He played Lancelot at his old school.”

Rachel, who thought Mike lived in a crack house, got a dreamy look on her face and said, “How totally romantic. I could stand to be Guinevere to his Lancelot.”

“So the scary bit is just an act?” Sami asked.

“As far as I can tell,” I said.

She was quiet for a moment, playing with her carrot sticks. “I need to tell you something,” she said.

“What?” I barely knew her, what could she have to tell me? That she had standards too, like Lauren, and thinking Mike was nice was enough reason not to associate with me?

“I think I know who took Trevor’s iPod.”

The clue! The missing piece of the puzzle! “Who?”

“Your sister.”

“Sara? But why?”

Sami took a deep breath. "All I know is she was rooting around in Trevor's jacket before he discovered it missing. But it didn't make any sense, because she was helping him look for it. I could be wrong. But I thought you should know."

"Yeah. Thanks." I crumpled up my lunch bag. None of this made any sense. I needed to talk to Sara, but I wouldn't see her until rehearsal.

When I got to Trig, I had no intention of stopping by Lauren's desk. But she stopped me.

"You blew us off at lunch," she said.

"I thought you had standards," I said and took my seat.

****

Rehearsal followed a different format today. Instead of proceeding with where we were in the script, like we had been doing, the choreographer was there and we worked on dances.

While the nuns were learning how to dance to "Maria" I sought out Sara. Trevor was sitting on the other side of her.

"I need to talk to you," I said.

"To me?" Sara said. "Or to him?"

Like I had anything to say to Trevor at this point. "To you. Alone."

Sara shrugged. "This isn't really a good time for that. How about later?"

I grabbed her by the arm and started to pull her up. "How about now?"

"Okay. Fine."

I led her to the back of the auditorium where we could sit and not be overheard. But should I just come right out and tell her she was spotted taking the iPod? Wouldn't she just deny an outright accusation? I had to lead into this. Make her admit it.

"You seem to be having a good time in the play," I said.

"Is this what this is about? Fine, say 'I told you

so,' and let me go."

"I wasn't going to say 'I told you so,'" though I'd like to. I tried again. "And you and Trevor seem to be getting along quite well."

"No thanks to you," she said with a sneer.

"Isn't it easier with me out of the way?" I asked.

"You'd think so, wouldn't you, but breaking up with you put him in a bad mood," she answered.

I can't say I was sad to hear that.

"Why'd you have to start liking Mike, instead?"

"I didn't start liking Mike, instead," I said. Though once I got to know him some, I did start liking him. But it hadn't meant that I stopped liking Trevor and none of it mattered anymore anyway: neither of them liked me.

"Then why did you kiss him at the dance?"

I was so tired of this subject. One stupid little kiss had caused so much trouble—and it hadn't even been on purpose. "I didn't mean to."

"How do you accidentally kiss someone?" Sara asked skeptically.

"You'd be surprised," I answered, trying not to think of Mike's kisses.

"Anyway, I've never accidentally kissed someone," Sara said. "When I kiss someone it's on purpose."

I honestly wished I could say the same.

"Everything would have been so much better if you had just let everyone think Mike stole the iPod. Then he'd have been kicked out of the play. That's what Trevor wanted."

"Why do you care what Trevor wanted?" I asked. But before she had a chance to answer I asked another question. "Is that why you took the iPod, because Trevor wanted you to?"

"He didn't know about it. Not at first." She clapped her hand over her mouth as she realized what she had admitted.

"Emma, Sara," Mrs. Valente called from the

stage, “we need you up here for ‘The Lonely Goatherd’.”

“You’ve got to tell Mrs.Valente,” I said to Sara as we headed toward the stage.

“Not a chance,” Sara said.

“People still think Mike took it.”

Sara grinned a little. “The only people who believe him now think you’re a slut. Pretty funny.”

Hysterical. “Tell. Or I will,” I said.

“No. You won’t,” she said.

We were at the stage steps now. And I sighed as she moved ahead of me to get on stage. She was right. I wouldn’t tell. I just had to figure out a way to get Sara to tell. But for the next fifteen minutes we were busy sorting out the choreography for ‘The Lonely Goatherd’ and I couldn’t formulate a plan.

Next the choreographer wanted to work on “So Long, Farewell,” which was a song I wasn’t in, but Sara was.

I sat by myself in the audience, trying to think of a way to get Sara to admit to taking the iPod. Unfortunately, as the “children” all cuckoo-ed their way through the song, I couldn’t think of anything.

Sami sat down next to me. “So, did she take it?”

“What? Oh. Yeah, she did.”

“Any idea why?”

“Something about wanting to make Trevor happy.” I sighed. “Now I just have to make her admit it.”

“She likes Trevor, huh?”

“I guess.”

Sami nodded a few times. “I have an idea.”

“Emma,” Mrs. Valente called, “we need you on stage.” Of course they did. So I couldn’t find out what Sami’s plan was. I did see her deep in conversation with some of the other nuns though. Maybe they were part of her plan? Were they going to dress up in their nun’s habits and get Sara to admit it out of good old-fashioned Catholic guilt?

When we finished practicing the next song, Sami approached Mrs. Valente. She didn't keep her voice low and quiet. She spoke as if she planned on being overheard. "I know who took Trevor's iPod," she said.

This was her plan? She was just going to flat out tell on Sara? But Sara would just deny it. That would never work.

"Why didn't you tell me earlier?" Mrs. Valente asked.

"I wasn't sure if what I saw made sense."

"Well, what did you see?"

Everyone was watching now, waiting to see what Sami was going to say. The blood had all drained from Sara's face. She didn't look good at all.

"Trevor did it." Sami said.

Everyone gasped. Even me. This was not what had happened. Why would she lie about that? What was the point of getting Trevor in trouble? I might not be too happy with him right now, but that didn't mean I wanted him to get in trouble for something he didn't do. That was no better than Mike getting in trouble for something he didn't do.

Sara gasped loudest of all.

Mrs. Valente turned to Trevor who was still sitting in the auditorium, his mouth gaping open. "Is this true, Mr. McGrath?"

"No!" But it was Sara who said it. "It wasn't Trevor. He didn't know about it."

All heads swiveled toward Sara. "Didn't know about what?" Mrs. Valente asked gently.

"I took it." Sara said.

Sami looked at me and gave me a half-smile. She'd gotten Sara to admit it. She was good.

"I guess I didn't see what I thought I saw," Sami said.

"Why?" Mrs. Valente asked Sara.

"To get Mike kicked out of the play," Sara said quietly. She hung her head; all the earlier bravado she had shown me was gone.

"Why on earth would you want to do that?" Mrs. Valente was apparently oblivious to the undertones around here.

"It's what Trevor wanted."

Now all heads turned back to Trevor who had stood up and was approaching the stage. "I just thought the play would be better off without him," Trevor said. "He doesn't exactly look like the ideal St. Stephen's student."

Mrs. Valente took her glasses off as if to get a better look at Trevor. "Here at St. Stephen's we don't judge people by appearances."

"Yes, we do," Lauren said, from her seat in the front row. "That's why we have to wear uniforms and everything, so everyone looks alike."

"That's not the only reason for uniforms. It's to remind you that there is more behind the appearance." Mrs. Valente put her glasses back on and said, "Trevor, Sara, I'd like to talk with both of you in the hallway please. Miss Davis, will you please direct them through the next song?"

"I was going to do 'Sixteen Going on Seventeen' next," she said.

Mrs. Valente sighed and tapped her foot. "Pick something else."

She picked one of the songs with the nuns. The rest of us sat in the audience and watched. Lauren sat down next to me. "Hey, um, are you going to the Snack Shack after the rehearsal?"

"Didn't think I measured up to your standards."

"I think we need to reassess our standards."

"You think?" I wasn't ready to forgive and forget quite yet.

"You can ask Mike to come too," she said.

"Mike doesn't want to spend time with me. He won't even talk to me."

"Maybe that will change now that everyone knows he really wasn't responsible."

Maybe. But, I didn't have high hopes.

Mrs. Valente came back in from the hallway with Sara and Trevor. None of them looked particularly happy. "That will be all for today," she called out. "Tomorrow we'll start with the first scene of act II. Study your scripts and be ready."

I looked at my watch. Only three o'clock. An early day today. Maybe it would be a good day for the Snack Shack. And maybe I could ask Mike. But once again, he was already leaving by the time I looked for him.

"Just take me home," Sara said to Jake as we put on our coats. Her eyes were red and puffy.

"What did Mrs. Valente do?" Jake asked.

"Three day in-school suspension and no school activities for those three days. That means no rehearsal for the rest of the week for me." Sara headed toward the exit and we followed.

"Did Trevor get punished?" I asked.

Sara turned and threw me a dirty look. "No. You'd like that wouldn't you?"

"No!" I insisted. "I don't want him in trouble. I don't want you in trouble either."

Trevor rushed up to us then and pulled Sara aside. I couldn't hear what he said, but when he left, she was smiling. She turned to me as we headed to Jake's car. "At least he appreciates what I did for him. He asked me to the movies on Friday."

Lauren put her arm around my shoulder. "I think you and I need a trip to the Snack Shack."

I looked at her and smiled. "I think you're right."

So, while Jake took Sara home, and Caitlyn had to wait around for the late bus, Lauren and I walked over to the Snack Shack. "I missed you," she said as we sat in one of the tiny booths. It wasn't often we weren't there with a crowd.

"I missed you too," I said.

"I figure, if you want to be friends with a loser, that's okay. I still want to be your friend." She grinned, letting me know she was teasing.

"You're lucky I believe friends stick by each other. No matter what."

Lauren ducked her head so her hair hid her face. "You're right. I am lucky." She opened her menu.

"What are you looking at the menu for?"

"I thought we could branch out. They must sell something here that's not nachos or cheesy fries."

We settled on mozzarella sticks. We didn't talk about the past couple of days, that wasn't our style. We talked about everything else. It was good to have my best friend back.

"So tomorrow we do the first scene of act II," Lauren said as we were getting ready to leave.

"Yup," I agreed as I counted out the tip.

"The scene where you have to kiss Mike," Lauren said.

The scene where I had to kiss Mike.

Chapter 15
"Till You Find Your Dream"

On stage the "children" played blind man's bluff with "Max" as they sang some of "The Lonely Goatherd." But as I stood in the wings and watched, all I could think about was the coming scene where Mike and I had to kiss.

And I really wanted to kiss him again. But I wanted him to want it too. What if he'd written me off completely? What if I could never redeem myself in his eyes? A couple of weeks ago I had barely given Mike a second thought and now he was all I could think about.

Did that mean I was falling in love? I didn't remember feeling this way about Trevor. We'd always had fun together and enjoyed doing things with each other, but I don't remember this obsessive wondering what he was thinking about.

Love was too big a word. Maybe I was falling in *like*. No, like wasn't big enough. Maybe it was love.

It didn't make any sense to fall in love with Mike now. Not now that he didn't even like me anymore. But maybe I could get a second chance, if I could ever get him to speak to me.

"Sara was responsible, huh?"

I looked up startled to see Mike standing next to me. He wasn't looking at me; he was watching the action on the stage instead, but at least he was talking to me.

"She was," I said, trying to keep my voice low-key and nonchalant, which was hard when my heart was suddenly beating a million beats a minute. He was talking to me again. Maybe I would get that second chance after all. I just couldn't blow it.

"Why?" he asked.

"She did it for Trevor. He was jealous. He thought I was falling for you." Had I actually said that? My face burned. I couldn't look at him.

"And are you?" he asked quietly.

Yes. I needed to say yes. But before I could make my voice work Lauren had grabbed him by the arm.

"That's our cue, Captain," she said.

And arm in arm, they went on stage as the Captain and Elsa. I had a few more pages of dialogue to wait. Lauren was only on stage for about two minutes, and then she and Jake exited and sat in a quiet corner, arms around each other, until they had to be on stage again.

This play was working out quite well for them. They got to be on stage together, they got to be off stage together. They had lots of time to just be together. It was supposed to be like that for me and Trevor. Could it be that way for me and Mike?

I watched Mike now as he rehearsed his scene. I really wanted to be friends with him. No—I wanted to be more than friends. Was that asking too much?

Mike came off stage, which meant I had to go on in a minute.

"Mike," I said as he passed me.

He turned to look at me. I couldn't just baldly answer his question from before. Not when I didn't know how he felt about me at all.

"I'm really sorry. For everything," I said.

Mike nodded, gave a small smile, winked at me, and it was my cue. I needed to start singing off stage. Had that smile and wink meant that he forgave me for my role in the mess?

Did it mean that maybe he'd kiss me again sometime? I entered the stage, on cue, singing happily. A few lines of dialogue and then Mike was beside me.

"*You've come back*?" he asked, as the Captain.

But his eyes were pure Mike and they were boring into me. And the question wasn't for Maria. It was for me, Emma. And I answered it, the only way I could.

I said my next line.

"*Yes, Captain.*" I hoped he would understand that the yes wasn't only Maria's, but mine as well.

He continued, complaining that Maria had left without saying goodbye.

As Maria, again, I answered. And my "forgive me" was more mine than Maria's.

"*Why did you do this to us? Tell me,*" Mike/Captain asked.

Maria had left the Captain because she was afraid that she was in love with him. But what was my reason? Why had I not stood up for him? Why had I betrayed him in that way? Because I didn't want Trevor—or anyone—to know how I felt about Mike.

But I did have strong feelings for Mike, and now I didn't care if everyone knew it—not even Trevor.

"*Please don't ask me,*" I answered, as Maria. "*Anyway, the reason no longer exists.*"

"*Then you're back to stay?*" Mike asked.

I wanted to say yes. To tell him I didn't want to walk away from him again. I didn't like the feeling I'd gotten when he'd looked so hurt, when I had kept silent. But I was still in character, and I had to say that I would only stay until they got a new governess.

A few more words exchanged and then I left the stage, while Jake and Lauren came back on.

I threw myself onto the backstage sofa. What had happened out there? Was it my imagination, or were we really having a conversation using the words of the play?

Maybe it was my imagination. Maybe everything with Mike was just illusion. What did I have to go on anyway? There was the kiss at the dance. That kiss should have never happened. That had been an awesome kiss. There was the afternoon at his house. I'd enjoyed being with him, even if it had been awkward. There was the kiss backstage. That had been another awesome kiss.

But was that all there was to it? Did we just have a physical thing—good kisses but nothing else? But there *was* more to it. There was the way my stomach felt as if it had fallen through the floor when I had hurt Mike that time. It hurt my heart to see him hurt. That had to be because of more than the fact that he was a good kisser.

He was a good kisser though.

Jake and Lauren and Mike were singing their song now. I loved this song about a "crazy planet full of crazy people" that all revolves around "me." It was lively and fun and—not true, was it?

The world doesn't revolve around any one of us individually. We are all connected in some way. What we do affects others. I kissed Mike and hurt Trevor. I tried to shield Trevor from what I'd done and hurt Mike. Sara tried to please Trevor and caused all sorts of trouble. It was all a big messy muddle, but it was all connected—not simply each person being the center of their own universe—like the song indicated.

They finished the song and Jake exited. Now it was just Mike and Lauren again—and time for my entrance. Soon Mike and I were the only ones on stage.

And he looked at me with those deep blue eyes and my stomach did flip-flops. How could I have thought he was not my type? How could there be anyone better suited for me than him?

We said our lines, being the Captain and Maria, careful with each other.

I said, "*The Mother Abbess, she said that you have to look for your life.*"

Was that what I was doing? Was I looking for

my life? And what was I finding? That in order to find out anything I had to look deep. I had to look beyond the easy fix, look beyond first impressions.

"*Often, when you find it, you don't recognize it,*" he said as Captain.

How very true. I had run into Mike on audition day, and never realized that our lives would be so intertwined, and that I would want them to be.

"*Then one day,*" he said, "*one night, all of a sudden, it stands before you.*"

"*Yes,*" I managed to breathe out. It was my line, but it was also me speaking. Yes. You don't know what you are looking for until it is standing right in front of you. I didn't know it was Mike I wanted until he was right there, in front of me.

"*I look at you now, and I realize this is not something that has just happened,*" Mike said the Captain's lines. "*It's something I've known, deep inside me, for many weeks...You knew it, too! What was it that told you?*"

My stomach felt like it was down somewhere below my knees. I didn't know how to answer this.

How did I know that I was falling in love with Mike? Because I was. I couldn't deny it any longer. Luckily, I realized I didn't actually have to answer the question. I had the answer. In the script in my hand.

"*Brigitta,*" I answered. "*She said—when we were dancing that night...*" I remembered that dance, not the one in the play, the one in the school gym. I remembered being in Mike's arms. I remembered the feel of his lips on mine. My heart was beating too fast.

"*...That was not just an ordinary dance,*" Mike answered. And I knew he was thinking of that night as well.

And then we were up to the lines that were the prelude to the kiss; the kiss that we had barely been able to get through the other day. Mike said his line and moved closer to me. So close, I could feel his breath on my face.

And then he kissed me. And it was a kiss just as wonderful as that one on the dance floor. Maybe better. My arms were around him. I was kissing him back. This moment could last forever.

Except that it didn't.

Mrs. Valente cleared her throat. Loudly. And I remembered we were on stage. At rehearsal.

We broke apart to a smattering of applause and catcalls from the cast members in the audience.

"*It is different*," I said my line. But I was so deliriously happy I didn't think I could contain it. I couldn't keep my happiness in. I wanted to shout for joy and laugh and dance and sing.

Luckily, I got to sing, because there was a song now. And I sang it to Mike—sang about being an ordinary couple, moving through life arm in arm, kissing each other every morning and every night.

How could I have ever thought that "Sixteen Going on Seventeen" was a romantic song? This song was the most wonderful love song I could ever imagine.

We finished our song and, hand in hand, left the stage.

"Was that real?" I asked Mike as soon as we were in the wings, almost afraid that it was all a trick of my imagination and he was going to tell me that he was just acting.

"It felt real to me," he answered.

"Me too," I answered.

"Okay, that will wrap it up for today. I'll see all of you tomorrow," Mrs. Valente called from out front.

"Let's go somewhere," Mike said. Our hands were still clasped together.

"Sounds good," I said.

We headed out to the front. Jake and Lauren were putting their coats on.

Jake shook his head when he saw me. "That was

some Public Display of Affection, little sis."

I just grinned. "I don't know what you're talking about. We were just following the script."

"So, what's the script say you do now?" Lauren asked, smiling indulgently at me.

I looked at Mike and smiled. "It says we ride off into the sunset on his motorcycle."

"How about just riding as far as the Snack Shack?" Lauren suggested.

Mike shrugged.

"Okay," I agreed. I didn't really care where we went, as long as we went together.

And when I was on the back of Mike's motorcycle, and we headed west toward the Snack Shack, I realized that we were heading into the setting sun.

And it seemed absolutely perfect.

Thank you for purchasing this Wild Rose Press publication. For other wonderful stories of romance, please visit our on-line bookstore at www.thewildrosepress.com.

For questions or more information contact us at info@thewildrosepress.com.

The Wild Rose Press
www.TheWildRosePress.com